ONE EYED JACK

By Christopher J. Lynch

The characters and events in this book are purely fictional. Any similarity to real persons, living or deceased is purely coincidental.

ISBN: 1475174438
ISBN-13: 978-1475174434

DEDICATION

To all of those who never stopped believing in me.

One Eyed Jack Video Trailer:
http://www.youtube.com/watch?v=Ydvb5XTXEGE
&feature=youtu.be

ACKNOWLEDGMENTS

Special thanks to:

Erik Gebhard of ALTAVEST Worldwide Trading Inc. for his assistance in understanding the world of commodities trading.

John Lynch for his tireless work and technical expertise in designing the Yoursercretsaresafe.com website.

Rob McLendon, AlhpaLens Productions, Director of Photography and Editor of the One Eyed Jack Video Trailer, for creating a great movie and saving me from myself.

Kate Stewart, Ebook editing 4 U, for having a keen eye, tons of patience, and a big eraser.

Cover art by Digital Donna: http://digitaldonna.com/

Cover snakeskin eye patch courtesy Gamble Gifts: http://www.gamblesgifts.com/

ONE

I make my living by keeping secrets.

Actually, I make it by letting others' keep theirs.

That's right, I'm that guy. The blackmailer, the extortionist, the guy you never see and wish you had never heard from. I'm the one who sees into the dark corners of your soul, the parts of your life you want to remain hidden.

Fancy yourself a religious man who attends church every Sunday, but who has a propensity for porn shops the other six days of the week? Don't worry; the congregation will never know as long as you keep tithing into my collection plate. Let's call it a "Sin Tax."

Got a shady lawyer pushing a bogus personal injury suit through the courts for you? You'll get your settlement - as long as I get my cut.

An extra-marital affair with your secretary? You guessed it; pay the piper.

All and all, it's a decent living. Please note that I'm using the adjective as it applies to monetary as opposed to moral terms. But, it's not an easy trade, and it has its share of risks. I've had my nose broken twice, my ribs fractured, and have had any number of close encounters with automobiles that came speeding out of nowhere trying to kill me.

But I could usually figure out who did it. And then, of course, all of the dirty little secrets would come out, and in living color. I'm sure I've been the cause of numerous divorces over the years, as well as terminations of employment, and plenty of fraud convictions. But that's how you keep people honest; you make them pay up.

And if you think I'm a slime, at least I'm a slime with good manners. Allow me to introduce myself. My name is John Sharp, a.k.a. "One Eyed Jack", a moniker I assure you wasn't the result of a birth defect or running recklessly through the house with a pair of scissors. Several years back I made the mistake of not researching one of my targets very carefully. He was a plastic surgeon in Beverly Hills who had a predilection for young male prostitutes. He had a very successful practice, a couple of nice houses, a trophy wife, and several country club memberships. He was, as I liked to say, my kind of man; "a man with a lot to lose".

What I hadn't figured on was the fact that one of his patients happened to be a Russian Mafioso who was on the lam and having his identity altered by the good doctor. The doc had his Mafioso client sick his pit bulls on me and the next thing I knew I was being informed that I saw way too much of this world, and that the situation would soon change. I woke up a couple of hours later in the hills above Los Angeles and found I was seeing a lot less, fifty percent if you want to do the math.

* * *

Hawthorne, California was a densely populated suburb located in the southwest end of Los Angeles County. It was a blue-collar town of modest homes, easy access to freeways, and convenient shopping. The Los Angeles International Airport was within earshot of the town, and the noise and congestion it spawned had not only driven down property values, but also given rise to numerous low-rent motels. The Peacock Motel was just one of these establishments.

Low-slung and non-descript, the Peacock was the sort of place you never really noticed. It was set back off the main boulevard just far enough that you could easily miss it if you weren't paying attention. The parking lot was along the side of the building, and several overgrown Magnolia trees offered copious amounts of shade but more importantly, cover. People could reasonably assume that no one would spot them as they pulled into the parking lot, exited their cars, and took up residence for an hour or so. People felt safe here, and anonymous. People felt they could get away with anything at the Peacock.

But people were often wrong.

I happened to consider the Peacock a bit like my own little happy hunting ground; a lair of lust well stocked with a steady stream of those escaping sexual boredom. The owner, Amit, a Pakistani national, was beholden to me and served as my own little safari guide, advising me when new quarry happened to be on the prowl.

It just so happened that I had done a little research into Amit's brother-in-law and co-owner of the Peacock, Habib. I struck upon the fact that Habib had overstayed his student visa. As a foreigner from a desperate and limiting third world nation, our Habib felt – as many others before him had - that he might as well just stay in the good old land of opportunity to stake his claim and realize the American dream.

I presented this fact to Amit and obliquely reminded him that in a post 9-11 world, a dark complexion and turban did not bode well for someone who had overstayed their welcome. Presented with this fact – and the documentation to back it up – our friendly Pakistani proprietor immediately launched into the standard medley of denials, admissions, threats, pleas, cajoles, and finally, groveling. Eventually, he offered a substantial amount of money. This would have been the easy route for me to take, but like all successful entrepreneurs, I realized that I had to continually re-invest in order to grow my business.

To this end I offered up a rather elegant deal to my fellow businessman; I would keep mum regarding his brother-in-law's dubious immigration status, and he would feed me a continual stream of leads regarding those who had chosen to go outside the bounds of matrimony.

Amit was incensed at having to strike such a deal with the infidel and let loose with a stream of expletives in Urdu that I'm sure suggested I perform an anatomical impossibility. But in the end he was a practical man, and we agreed he would contact me as fresh game arrived. I had watched the Peacock long enough to know that one or two new regulars a month would not be an unreasonable quota to expect from him.

It was a Tuesday morning, just after 7:00 a.m. and Rosecrans Avenue was jammed with cars heading in both directions as people dropped their kids off at school or headed in to work. I was parked in a vacant dirt lot just next to the Peacock. The lot held several rows of cars that some enterprising person had plastered with "For Sale" signs. I had a set of similar signs in my vehicle for just such eventualities and had taped them to my side windows thirty minutes earlier. From here I had a perfect view of the motel parking lot, the office, and most importantly, all the doors to the rooms.

My vehicle of choice for these "Sneak and Peeks" was a 2002 Ford Windstar Mini-Van. It was light blue in color, faded, scratched, and looked like about a million others on the road. People couldn't stand to look at it, let alone remember it.

And even if someone were to take notice of it and copied down the plate number, they would quickly discover that it was registered to "Clive's Used Auto Sales" and was carried on the dealership's inventory list. It seems old man Clive had a sweet little set-up with "Ace Speedometer Service" where, for a fee, and through the use of a master reset chip and a bootleg program, Ace could sweep back the miles on an electronic odometer, thus increasing the sale price of the vehicles. Virtually every heap Clive unloaded on his unsuspecting patrons had had its mileage "cut", a crime that carries with it federal penalties and jail time, along with the seizure of the business and all of its assets.

I showed Mr. Clive a list of VIN numbers that had suffered this nefarious fate and he readily cut a deal. I could have full and unrestricted use of the mini-van while he maintained the title, registration, and insurance. All and all, it was a very tidy set-up.

And before you think Ace Speedometer got off the hook painlessly; I'm into them for four bills a month lest the beans get spilled and they join old Clive in the poky. The four hundred comes in handy and just about covers my fuel costs.

At about 7:10 AM a woman in a late model silver Camry pulled into a spot in the parking lot of the Peacock. I had been given a heads up on the vehicles to watch for, as well as the standard time of these trysts. I was seated in the middle seat of the mini-van behind a Canon XL-H1 with a 6X HD zoom. It was mounted on a tripod that bolted to the floor. A Fire Wire connected it to a laptop on the seat next to me, and gave me a real-time view on the laptop's screen. The camera was aimed through the van's windshield, and had been rolling for the past couple minutes, capturing the Camry as it pulled into the lot and parked.

I peered into the viewfinder and adjusted the controls to zoom into a close-up of the license plate. I held it there for several seconds before widening back out. The camera's date/time clock was running, but I always kept the van's radio on as well. It was tuned to a local news station that gave the time, weather and traffic conditions every couple of minutes. This was picked up on the camera's audio track. I found that the sound of the newscaster's voice added another level of authenticity to the tape.

The woman in the Camry stayed put and made no motion to exit the vehicle. Through the rear window of the vehicle, I could see the silhouette of her as she raised her two arms level with her shoulders and made a pulling motion between her hands. I had seen this same motion enough times before to know what was going on; she was removing her wedding ring.

A few minutes later, a dark blue Ford pickup pulled into the lot and swung in quickly next to the space occupied by the Camry. The driver's door opened a few seconds later and a man in his late forties to early fifties came lumbering out. He was a big man with fleshy features: arms, chest, neck, head. He was dressed in khaki slacks and a rust colored golf shirt. The shirt was wrinkled and untucked in the back. If he was wearing a belt I couldn't see it, as everything seemed to sag over his waist like bread dough over the lip of a bowl. He had dark curly hair going gray, and dark challenging eyes. Through the viewfinder I caught the look of a puffy, reddened face that had never missed last call. A half-smoked cigar hung loosely from his lips. He took a quick look out to the street and then to the lot where I was stationed. I didn't move a muscle and he never saw me watching him. His eyes said that they didn't care if I did; he couldn't give a shit about what the rest of the world thought about him.

He angled toward the Peacock's tiny office and glanced over at the Camry briefly. He shot a knowing smirk to the woman inside, and then he continued on to the office.

While he was checking in, I took the time to zoom in tight on the truck's license plate. The woman in the Camry still had not budged, nor did I expect her to until the last moment; that's just the way women were in this sort of thing.

I panned back out and was able to take in the whole scene: both cars, the man in the office, and the line of doors to the rooms that faced the vacant lot where I was stationed.

The man finally emerged from the office tossing a key in his hand. That was how backward the Peacock was; the doors to the rooms still used keys instead of cards. He spat out his cigar on the pavement and didn't bother to step on it to crush it out. He reached a door to a room just to the left of the spot where the two cars were parked and jammed the key into the deadbolt. From where I sat, I would have a perfect shot of the two of them.

As soon as the door to the room opened, the woman's car door flew open like a loose shutter in a windstorm and she made a beeline to the room, as fast as you could make a bee-line hobbling in high heels. She stopped just long enough to click her key-fob and the Camry blinked and honked.

She was about the same age as the man but dressed much nicer and more professional. She had on a nice light gray business suit with a white blouse and black heels. Her hair was blond and well coifed, and I could imagine her several hours after this rendezvous standing in front of a bored crowd cycling through a presentation of PowerPoint slides.

I zoomed in closer on the two of them, and was tight-in when she made one last quick turn to look around to see if anybody had spotted them. It was a crucial mistake as I captured an irrefutable image of her face as she looked back toward the camera.

Bingo!

They entered the room quickly and the door slammed shut. I could almost hear the deadbolt being slid closed.

I shut off the camera after a few seconds and watched as the laptop continued rendering the stream. I had a high-end program that I used with a fast sampling time. After a few keystrokes, the first of the DVDs began burning. As this was going on, I began disconnecting the camera from its tripod, and then the tripod from the floor.

The first DVD ejected and I popped another blank into the tray. I stowed the camera just as the second DVD finished burning.

I took each of the DVDs and put them into the special sleeves I had printed up for just such occasions. The sleeves read:

Contact me at:
http://www.yoursecretsaresafe.com *if you don't want these to be made public. You have 24 hours.*

I exited the mini-van and strode over to the Peacock parking lot. As I got closer to the rooms, I could hear the muffled groans of the man as he went at it just a few feet away.

After carefully placing a DVD under the windshield wiper of each of the subject's cars, I turned back toward the vacant lot and to the rows of cars.

Just as I was getting close to the lot, I could see the head of a man bobbing through the glass of some of the vehicles as he walked between the rows. He had cut over into the row I was parked in and was heading straight towards my van. He might have been someone just checking out the vehicles, but the hairs on the back of my neck stood up. Something didn't feel right about the way he was moving.

I cut into the gap between the van's driver door and the other cars, and we came face to face.

"Shit!"

His name was Troy Harper; thirty-seven years old, married, two children, good job, and with an addiction to young prostitutes. He had found a DVD on his windshield after patronizing the discreet services of the Peacock about two months ago. He was on the hook for three bills a month and had vowed to track me down and kill me. In his hand was an aluminum baseball bat. I didn't see a softball in his other hand, and I didn't think he was looking for a pick-up game.

"You son of a bitch!" he hissed.

He was a tall, lanky man with an angular face and a nose that said he had bobbed when he should have weaved. His gray eyes were cold with vengeance as he stomped toward me, his footfalls kicking up dust with every step. He was dressed in blue jeans and a light blue work shirt with his name over the left pocket. He had on a denim jacket that was unbuttoned and open across the chest. I judged the distance between us to be about a car-length and a half, and closing fast. When he was even with the back of my van, I reached into my jacket, pulled the unit out, squared myself, and took aim at the gap between his jacket. I fired.

Two steel darts shot out of the front of the Taser gun. Thin wires, the thickness of a cat's whiskers, trailed behind them. The report was no louder than a child's cap gun, and no one would hear it above the sound of the traffic that roared by.

The darts hit him mid-torso and penetrated his skin. Sharp barbs on the tips of the darts held them in. Instantaneously, electrical pulses designed to mimic and interrupt the neural and motor skill centers of the brain began pulsing at fifteen to twenty cycles per second.

His body jerked into convulsions, arms flying out from his sides as if drawn by invisible strings. The bat slammed into the side of a black Infinity, putting a nice dent in the side panel and instantly reducing the car's resale value. It dropped from his hand as his body twisted and corkscrewed into the ground helplessly. I let go of the trigger and stepped toward him, kicking the bat away from him in the process. Saliva dribbled down his chin and a growing wet spot had formed in his crotch.

"Your three-hundred dollars a month just doubled asshole! Try this shit again and the video of you with those girls will be on the internet in a matter of minutes!"

I hit the trigger one last time for good measure, pulled out the darts, and headed back to the van.

Like I said before, this wasn't an easy trade.

TWO

In the craft of extortion, there are essentially four phases of the work process:

Research and Discovery – Finding the individual, or individuals, who are engaged in the questionable activities.

Capture - Recording and documenting these activities so that they are irrefutable and adequately embarrassing or incriminating to the individual(s) if made public.

Contact– The anonymous presentation to the individual(s) of the documentation along with the instructions and terms for the maintenance of discretion.

And finally, Collection – Essentially an accounts receivable and bookkeeping function similar to a million other businesses.

After the Peacock, I headed westbound on Rosecrans Avenue toward Manhattan Beach, an upscale community of million dollar homes, trendy vehicles, and plenty of California casual excess. I maintained one of my many PO Boxes at the local post office and it was time to collect some payments. The morning rush-hour traffic had increased to the point to where it took two, sometimes three, cycles of the signal lights to get through the intersection, but this was what you put up with when you decided to live where seven million others want to.

I arrived at the Post Office a few minutes before eight and noted that a line had already formed at the door. People were clutching boxes and thick envelopes, and waiting anxiously for the doors to open as if their parcels held the key to world peace, or a cure for cancer. I parked in the lot across the street and looked at my watch. I thought that she might not be in Pre-op yet, and decided to risk a call. I pulled out the cell phone I used for personal calls and dialed. She answered in two rings.

"Hello sweetie," I said before she could speak.

"Hello slacker," she replied by way of playful insult.

"Slacker," I cried, trying my best to sound wounded. "I treat you every day as if it's Valentine's Day and this is the thanks I get?"

"Ha!" she laughed. "You treat me like your personal little Geisha every day! That's what I get for hooking up with one more guy with yellow fever."

She giggled playfully and then quickly added, "...not that I mind of course."

Her name was Naoko. She was Japanese, thirty-three years old, and a veterinarian. She came from a very good family of doctors and accountants in Hawaii. I had met her on a golf course about eighteen months ago. She was cute and petite, and the best thing to ever come into my life, the only thing in it that was pure and clean. In my world of scumbags, cheats, and grifters, it was refreshing just to have something to hold sacred, something to give you hope for humanity. She believed that I was a free-lance insurance investigator and I intended to keep it that way. It was one of the few lies I had ever told her.

"How are things going?" I asked. "Are you in Pre-Op yet?"

"Nah," she answered casually. "Bowzer's parents called and said that he threw up on the carpet right before they were getting ready to leave. Happens a lot with Border Collies; they're so smart and so in tune with the emotions of the owner, they know about as much as anybody else in the house about what's going on. They're cleaning it up right now. It's okay though, my assistant's running late anyway so the whole day's schedule is shot to hell."

"No time to meet for lunch then?" I offered.

"Not a chance. I'll be lucky if I can wolf down a Teriyaki chicken-wrap later on."

"We're still on for dinner though at my place?"

"Yes," she teased. "Your little Geisha will be there my Johnny-San."

"All-right," I said. "I'll have a little glass of favorite chilled Chardonnay waiting for you the minute you step through the door."

"OOOHH", she said. "Now you're talking slacker. You just may get your back walked on by my little feet tonight."

"Just no heels this time, OK?"

She giggled and I could hear some commotion in the background: voices, a dog barking, a door being slammed.

"The patient's here," she said. "Gotta run...MUUUAAAHHH!"

The connection went dead before I could "MUUUAAAHHH" her back. She had graduated with her degree in Veterinary Medicine from UC Davis six years ago and now worked with another veterinarian in Redondo Beach. The practice was thriving, and people loved Naoko's professionalism and calming bedside manners with their pets.

I slipped the phone back into the holster and looked up. The doors were being unlocked and people were pressing in like they were escaping the plague. I exited the car and headed across the street to the Post Office.

I used a re-mailing service in Texas that forwarded my mail to this, and several other PO Box addresses', thus insuring that none of my marks knew the correct address of the PO Boxes, my home address, phone numbers, personal e-mail address...or even my first name. Lesson number one in the business of keeping secrets: keep yours better than the other person keeps his.

There were four envelopes in the box when I opened it. Each had been sent to the re-mailing service, along with my account number on the bottom. I made a quick mental note of the four return addresses and knew whom they were from.

One was my cut of a settlement lien for a scammer who had claimed his back was injured lifting a crate of eggs in a supermarket. Yet another lesson, Dear Reader: Don't go out line dancing when you're trying to claim a damaged lumbar. It was nice and fat, and would be a one-time payment. I usually charged ten percent of the settlement, and this would come outside of the Attorney's thirty- three percent. The amount they were asking for was $120,000.00 and I figured they would settle for probably half that amount.

The second envelope was from a garment factory in downtown LA that kept in servitude any number of illegal immigrants toiling away to make the designer labels that you might be wearing at this very moment. They were on the hook for five bills a month if they wanted to keep their sweatshop humming along. It wasn't a lot of money considering the amount of business that they did, but I suspected that I wasn't the only one putting the pinch on them and didn't want to kill the cow by getting too greedy.

The third and forth were from two co-workers who were engaged in a romantic affair. Each had marriages, nice homes, and good jobs to lose in the local aerospace industry. Their twice weekly lunch time trysts were setting them back a couple hundred apiece to keep the compromising pictures of them from becoming public domain. The woman always paid up without question, but the man had been a hard case from the beginning. He had tried the standard insults, threats to find me and bash my skull in, pleas to drop the price, etc. None of these tactics ever worked on me, but it never stopped him from trying.

I tucked the envelopes into my pants pocket, closed the box door, and locked it. I never opened the envelopes inside the Post Office and instead waited to get into my car. The payments were all in cash; twenties, and were double sealed inside two envelopes. I could usually tell just by the thickness of them who was tithing correctly and who needed a friendly reminder. The one from hard case seemed different this time, thinner. I hoped he wasn't stupid enough to try to send me a money order again.

I climbed back into the mini-van, looked around, and began opening them, beginning with the accident settlement. Included in the envelope along with the money was a copy of the judgment. The insurance company had just coughed up twenty-five thousand dollars to a scammer who could do the Horseshoe Shuffle better than you or I. I had asked for hundreds due to the large amount, and that was what I got; all twenty-five of them. I smiled. It would be Naoko's birthday before I knew it and she had hinted - rather strongly, and not for the first time - that she really liked little white stones, the kind that you purchase by the karat. I continued on with the rest of the envelopes.

Just as I had figured, the sweatshop was up to snuff. The same was true with the woman in the extra-marital affair; she always paid up without question. I wrote the amounts down on the inside flap of the envelopes and would enter them later in the Excel sheet I kept for record-keeping purposes. Before being deposited or spent, the money would go through a special scanner I had that would check for counterfeits, as well as marked bills. I never had encountered marked bills, but occasionally a counterfeit would show up. I would mail half of the bill back and admonish the payee to be more careful, lest they want the US Treasury after them, as well as yours truly.

Just as I had feared, the envelope from Hard Case contained no money, just a news clipping roughly torn out of a newspaper. I pulled it out and looked at it. It was an obituary. I looked at the picture and read the name. It was Hard Case's wife, and listed the standard info: birth date, location, what she died from, (Ovarian Cancer), where she had worked, and how she left behind a loving husband, blah, blah, blah. Written across the photo and narrative in an angry pen were the words:

The bitch is dead now scumbag. Take those fucking pictures of me and shove them up your ass! I ain't giving you another fucking dime!

I looked at it for a long moment, considering. People died all the time. Still, this was Hard Case I was dealing with.

I tucked it back into the envelope and started the van. I was hungry and it was time for some breakfast.

THREE

The Good Stuff Restaurant in Hermosa Beach was located in a quaint, clunky little building set just off of the concrete boardwalk that separated the beach from the rest of the world. It served great food at a good price and had a loyal following of "beach regulars." I ate here at least three times a week and the waitresses knew me well enough to not bother with a menu.

I grabbed my usual spot in the back corner of the restaurant with my back to the wall. From here I could see the door, as well as everyone who walked, jogged, rode, roller-bladed, otherwise moved past the window. Call me paranoid, but when you're in a business where you routinely make people's lives miserable, you try not to take unnecessary chances.

"Hi Jack," the waitress said, as a cup of coffee was slid in front of me. "What'll it be today?"

Her name was Alex. She was twenty something and was like many of the others that worked here: cute, nubile, and attending college while she made her rent by waiting tables for characters like me. She was dressed in the requisite Good Stuff shirt that read; *"You are what you eat...so eat Good Stuff,"* black tights, and had a red headband drawn back on her head.

"Chicken Chile-Verde breakfast burrito," I said.

"I knew that," she teased as she pulled a setting from the pocket in her apron and spread it out in front of me. "Just wanted to see if you were awake this morning."

"Barely", I said, although I had been up since 4:30. I took a sip of coffee, my first of the day. It was heavenly.

She bounced away and I pulled the obit clipping from my pocket to study it further.

It was true that you could do just about anything with desk-top publishing software these days, but I didn't give Hard Case a whole lot of credit for paying attention to the details.

The first thing I did was turn it over and look at the backside. It had a partial article regarding a bond measure that was in the process of facing an uphill battle. So far, so good. Even if my mark had thought enough to put something on the back to give it authenticity, he wouldn't have been smart enough to have it fragmented by the offsets in column margins.

The second thing I looked at was the paper. Newspaper stock had evolved past the wood-particle-impregnated pulp-stock of the past, but it was still a low quality paper. You could get blank sheets in bulk from suppliers on-line, but again; I still wasn't ready to give him any credit for this.

I took the article and rubbed it vigorously between my fingers. Like the paper it was printed on, the inks used in the newspaper printing process were a low-cost variety made of mineral oil. Due to the fact it was not given adequate time to dry, it smudged and transferred onto your hands if you worked it well enough. In a few seconds I could feel a familiar slickness on my thumb and forefinger. So much for that.

I could have taken this material analysis further and gotten the loupe out of my car, but there were easier ways. I pulled my laptop out the computer bag, set it on the table, and fired it up.

It was a brand new, top of the line HP that I had bought used from a college dropout after he figured getting high was a better use of his time than getting ahead in this world. His parents - who had given it to him as a send-off gift, had thoughtfully registered it in his name, as well as all of the software loaded onto it, insuring that if anyone ever found the laptop or hacked into it, it could never be traced to me. I had a government issued secure air-card that I used to get to the net, and as a final security measure, used an offshore "spider" router service for any communications. This router kept my whereabouts so convoluted and in so many locations worldwide simultaneously, that it would take the resources of the NSA for any of my marks to find me. As terrified as any of them were to even speak to the local police about their illicit activities, I slept well at night knowing this was an unlikely scenario.

Before delving further into the obit affair, I replayed the video I had shot of the couple at the Peacock Motel. I fast forwarded to the close-ups of their license plates and jotted the numbers down on the napkin Alex had set at my table.

I closed the video and logged into one of my e-mail accounts. At any given time, I maintained dozens of Yahoo, Gmails, and Hotmail accounts. Each of my marks got a different e-mail account to use when they made initial contact. After the payments began, I would close that account, open another and notify them of the change.

There were several new e-mails in the "in-box" of this particular account, but I wasn't interested in them right now. Instead I fired off a quick note to a guy I was leaning on at the California Department of Motor Vehicles. He had discovered a glitch in the agency's software that allowed him to erase the "salvage" status of a vehicle's title and re-title it as clean. He had a nifty little side business going with a couple of used car dealers. That's right my friend; that certified "good as new" used car you're driving right now may just have been the middle player in a four car pile-up. Besides providing info such as the vehicle's registered owner, license number, address, and driving record to me free of charge and on demand, my friend was also on the hook for two bills a month as a token payment.

I typed in the plate numbers of the cars and hit send just as Alex returned to my table, her slender arms laden with my steaming plate of food.

"Here you go Jack," she announced as she set the plate in front of me.

"Thanks Alex."

She took in a quick glance into my coffee cup and retrieved the pot to refill it. A few moments later, I was set.

While my food was cooling, I returned to my browser and began pulling up some of the on-line obit archives maintained by newspapers. My buddy Hard Case lived close-by, in the city of Torrance, and he probably would have had his dear departed wife's notice in the local publications.

A quick search of the paper's obits revealed no such notice – at least within the past couple of months - and I quickly switched sites to that of the Los Angeles Times. A few minutes of searching The Times' archives garnered the same results: No Mrs. Hard Case.

I moved the laptop off to the side to give me some more room and took a healthy first bite of my burrito – as if any bite of a burrito could be healthy.

I didn't know of any other local papers where he might have posted it and quickly began to smell a rat. Between bites I turned over the obit and began to read the fragment on the bond measure. I had only skimmed it before and thought that if I could pick up a clue here or there, I might strike some pay dirt. In the last sentence, I found what I was looking for.

The fragmented line read: " -omers of the Redlands water district may expe –"

Bingo!

Old Hard Case had thought that he could pull a fast one all right. Redlands, California was located about sixty miles east and north of the South Bay area in another county. By bribing an employee of a mortuary into running a bogus obit in an out of the area paper, no one would recognize his wife's name and call to express their condolences, ask what they could do, etc. His wife would not have people stopping her on the street saying they had heard she had died, and how could this have happened, and where did they get the picture from, etc. In essence, no one would ever know – or think - she had died...no one except good old One Eyed Jack.

Pretty clever Hard Case...just not clever enough.

I re-read the fragment of the bond measure story once more just to make sure and then, satisfied, stuffed it back into my pocket and went back to finishing my burrito. While I was eating, my laptop pinged two separate times letting me know I had some new e-mails. I finished my breakfast and had Alex take the plate away and refill my coffee before returning my attention to the computer, and to a world that needed me.

The first was from an e-mail address I had never seen before, but was routed through my "Your Secrets Are Safe" website so I knew what it was. I opened it up and read the angry vilification.

You son of a bitch! I aint gonna pay you shit! You may know my plate number and have my picture but you don't know my name or where I live. Only the cops can get that info and I don't think you're a cop. So fuck off!!

So, my first mark from the Peacock had found his DVD, played it, went to the website and decided to go right onto the defensive: Not a problem. While the range of reactions from a new mark ran from outright acquiescence and sheepishness, to the extreme of death threats, my new pal was nothing to be concerned about.

I'll get back to you in a bit tough guy.

I closed the first e-mail and opened the second one, which was from my pal at the DMV. He had come through and sent me a PDF with the info on both of the marks. Perfect timing.

I copied the drivers license number of Mr. Tough Guy and then went into a new window and logged onto the Emperium website. It was a service used by journalists and insurance fraud investigators, and my access to it came courtesy of my previous employer. I pasted the number into the proper search field, hit "enter", and then waited a few moments.

As the hourglass tumbled, I took a look out the window and noted that the day had begun to clear. If I were lucky, I would be able to take in a bike ride today.

A few moments later, the data dump appeared in front of me. I had tough guy's name – William Henry Batty, his age – 52, as well as his address, employment history, his social security number, and his phone numbers. Other tabs would link me to his driving record, his medical record, his police record, and to any legal judgments for or against. I clicked on to the county clerk link and entered his social security number. He was married, as I had figured, and his wife's name was Allison Mary Batty, age forty-eight.

That was all I needed for now, and I cut and pasted the info into a Word doc. for later reference. I quickly repeated the process with the information on the female from the Peacock and was now set to deal with any eventualities they could throw at me.

I begged off on another refill of coffee as Alex set the check down in front of me. I paid it and added a generous tip.

I returned to Tough Guy's e-mail and let him have it in the reply.

"Dear Bill," I began, letting him know from the very first sentence that I held the cards. *"You are correct in assuming that I am not a cop...but that's where the accuracy of your suppositions end. Your full name is William Henry Batty. You were born on September 15Th. 1960..."*

I went on to tell him his social security number, his wife's name and age, and what cars he owned. What I neglected to tell my new friend was that by going to the website, mal-ware had now infected his computer. A R.A.T. (remote access terminal) would allow me to remotely control his computer and snoop around at will. Besides this, a key-logger program would copy all of his passwords whenever he logged into his e-mail, social networking sites, or purchased anything on line. I would compile a list of his contacts, as well as be able to read all of his incoming and outgoing mail. I could see and copy every file, document, and photo on his computer, and he would never know it was happening. Thank you Mr. Tough Guy.

I finished the e-mail by telling him that his secret was worth two hundred a month if he wanted me to keep quiet. I expected his first payment on the first of the month beginning next month. And if he chose not to play ball and continue the tough guy approach, then he could start looking for a good divorce attorney – and they didn't work for two hundred a month.

I hit send and watched as it went through. Next, I opened the file on Hard Case. I jotted down his home address and logged off. Walking out, I waved good-bye to Alex as she juggled three plates of food between two forearms. She replied by way of a nod because that was all that she could do. I got into my car and headed eastbound toward the city of Torrance. I had one more piece of the puzzle to put into place.

*　*　*

The city of Torrance was a diverse community of one hundred-fifty thousand with everything from upscale homes in flowery-named developments, to low rent and subsidized apartments in areas even the cats were afraid to prowl through at night. Besides this, the city was home to numerous retail businesses, as well as a high tech industry, and a mammoth refinery owned by the Champion Oil Company.

Casa de Hard Case was located midway down a short cul-de-sac in an impossible to follow series of short streets and dead-ends near the downtown area of the city. After stopping twice to let the GPS re-calculate, I finally found myself sitting in front of his house. The street was quiet and deserted. A few cars were parked in driveways and in the street, but no one was outside watering, pulling weeds, or flying kites. It was like being on the backlot of a movie studio where the facades faced out onto the street, and everything was as still and quiet as a cemetery.

I studied the house for a few moments before getting out. It looked to be your standard three bedroom, one and a half bath tract home. The paint appeared fresh, but the rain gutters where old and rusty. I knew just what to do.

I retrieved a clipboard and a tape measure from the toolbox of props I kept in the back of the mini-van. Next to the toolbox, I had a small file box with various order forms for painting contractors, driveway re-surfacers, landscapers, and other sundry homeowner services. I attached a stack of bid sheets for a rain gutter company onto a clipboard. They were left over from a company that had once been owned by some unscrupulous gypsies that I had leaned on for a while, before they decided to move out of the area and start a new scam.

I scrawled the address of Hard Case's house onto the top form and stepped up the brick walk towards the front door like it was my tenth house of the day and I was bored and wanted to change jobs. If anyone were to ask what I was doing here, I had been mistakenly given the wrong house number to measure for a new set of seamless whites.

I figured that Hard Case would have been at work right now, but I wasn't sure if I would run into his wife. She had retired two years ago from the school district where she had been employed as a librarian for twenty-seven years. If she appeared at the door alive, I could then claim an experience no less incredible than the parable of Lazarus of Bethany.

I pushed the doorbell and heard it's muffled sound through the front door. I waited a few moments, listening: no footsteps, no dogs barking viciously, no one yelling, "Just a minute!" as they wiped their hands or finished in the bathroom. The house sounded empty. I tried the chime again and had the same response. Not even the ghost of Mrs. Hard Case came forth rattling her chains.

"They're not home."

The sound came from behind me. I turned to see a woman about sixty years old with a small white dog on a leash. The dog had a pink bow on the top of its head and regarded me suspiciously.

"Oh," I said. "I thought they were going to be home. I was supposed to measure for some new rain gutters. Do you know when they'll be home?"

"Well Mr. Moore won't be home until after five, and his wife, not for a couple of weeks."

"Well that's a surprise," I said, always stunned at how easily people give up information about the whereabouts and schedules of their neighbors. "She's the one who called and scheduled the appointment."

As I spoke, I made a sham of looking at the form on my clipboard as if to double-check the name and appointment time.

"Well she's off on a cruise right now," the woman said. "Three weeks."

"A three week cruise!" I repeated as if envious. "Well, lucky her."

"Isn't she though," the woman gushed. Her dog had since lost interest in me and now was sniffing at a spot on the corner of the walk where ten thousand dogs had left their scent.

"Her husband gave it to her as a birthday present," she went on. "Isn't that just so thoughtful?"

I nodded my head vigorously.

"Yes," I said. "Thoughtful. Very thoughtful indeed."

*   *   *

On the drive back from Torrance, I calculated Hard Case's new obligation for his stunt. His payments would now double to four hundred a month if he wanted to keep the video of him and his side-dish as well as the obit from finding their way into his wife's suntanned hands. I had seen similar cons fail to persuade me in the past and I typically doubled the tithing. It was like dealing with children in a lot of ways.

"You don't want to mow the front lawn? Fine; now you can do the back lawn as well."

The gas gauge in the Windstar showed less than a quarter of a tank and I pulled into the first gas station I saw to fill it up. As the numbers fluttered rapidly by on the dispenser's readout in front of me, I realized woefully that the price had gone up again. This would make it the third increase in two weeks. I sighed and wondered if it would ever end.

Maybe I should have tripled Hard Case's payments.

FOUR

After dealing with the Hard Case mini-scam, I drove north towards Westchester, a bedroom community that is bordered on the south by the Los Angeles International Airport and on the west by the Pacific Ocean. I set up surveillance just down and across the street from US Taxpayer, Mr. John T. Gunther: gross income for the prior tax year - $119,032.76, adjusted gross income for the prior year - $42,712.95, federal income tax withheld - $947.53. I knew all of this because the chiseling Mr. Gunther had used the tax services of Mr. Sid Bienbalm CPA, a man who in the world of crooked accountants, was the equivalent of a demigod.

I had gotten wind of the income-sheltering wizardry of Mr. Bienbalm and decided to give him a trial run. I forged a bogus W-2, and went to him explaining that I was in over my head, and had to get out from under my tax obligations – in any way possible. He gave me a greasy smile, and promptly laid out his range of unique and helpful services for.

For a fee of $750.00, you got what was referred to as, the "C" plan. For this amount, our man Sid would take all of the dubious deductions that he thought he could possibly get away with that would be just shy of triggering an audit. Pretty standard stuff.

The next tier up was the "B" plan in which he would set up a bogus home business for me with which I would be able to deduct everything from paper clips, to meals, to laptop computers. I was expected to somehow tie this to some personal interest of mine such as photography or dirt bike riding. For a fee of $2000.00 I would receive no receipts or any other documentation to justify the enterprise. And if I got audited for it, oh well, I provided the info to poor old Sid. He just filled in the blanks and did the math.

The granddaddy of them all though was the much revered "A" plan, whereupon our crooked bean-counter would not just set me up as a struggling entrepreneur, but would also provide bogus receipts, invoices, business cards, etc. There were three "Home Businesses" to choose from depending on my taste: A printing business, a cabinet making business, or a welding shop. And if Uncle Sam smelled a rat and decided to pay me a visit? Not a problem; Sid's team of expert deception artists would show up a couple days prior to the audit with a moving van filled with all of the equipment and materials I would ever need to convince an overworked government agent that I was just one more struggling businessman. They would move it all in, set it up, and even throw around some welding slag or sawdust to make it look completely kosher. The price of the "A" plan was $5,000.00 and was for only the boldest or most desperate of tax cheats.

I listened absently as my financial savior went through all of this; I had already scoped it out and knew the details. Besides that, the digital recorder in my pocket was picking all of it up.

"So then," he said at the conclusion of his pitch. "What'll it be? "The A, B or C plan?"

"This," I replied as I produced the recorder and laid it on the desk in front of him. I had rewound it a bit in my pocket and hit the play button for him to hear. The voice emanating from the recorder was unmistakably his as he outlined in perfectly clear details his shenanigans designed to defraud the federal government of their entitled revenues.

Crooked as a zig-zag stitch, Sid was no martyr and would throw any one of his clients under the bus to save his own skin. A few minutes later we had a cozy little deal worked out whereupon he would feed me the names of his clients who had chosen the "A" plan and were in the queue for an audit. Two months after that meeting, I found myself in front of the first chiseler's home.

The van was due to arrive sometime between noon and two o'clock. I had been set up here since a little after eleven and it was almost one o'clock now. Nothing had happened yet other than Mr.

Gunther - AKA "The Chiseler" - stepping out of his house several times and looking up and down the street nervously. I had gotten some good shots of him as he did this, but it wouldn't make much difference to the IRS; you were just a number anyway.

I made use of the time by checking e-mails and the like. I also took care of some administrative tasks. I had moved the info on the woman at the Peacock into my Excel file along with her secret beau: Mr. Tough Guy.

Her name was Marion Teresa Holtzinger. She was forty-seven years old, married with one child, and worked as an accountant at Sunshine Foods in Culver City. I still had not heard from her, but that didn't give me pause. People typically found themselves in a tailspin when the hammer came down and they were terrified, confused, and occasionally sickened to the point of physical illness. I was that sure she would respond soon enough after running through the standard medley of scenarios that she thought might relieve her of any obligation to me. Like all of the others though, she would eventually find none that were viable or painless, and realize that she would have no choice but to play ball.

Tough Guy had e-mailed me back though, responding that he would begin his payments as per the instructions. Cooperation or not, he couldn't help but add to the e-mail a threat that if he ever found me in a dark alley, he would wring my little blackmailing neck. Take a powder Tough Guy.

I heard a deep rumbling coming from the street behind me like a wave of thunder rolling in. I glanced up into the rear-view mirror and saw a large white box van moving slowly up the street and checking addresses. Chiseler must have heard it too because he was out of his front door like a shot and waving his arms like he was doing semaphore. I started the video camera and caught all of his idiotic antics.

The van pulled up in front of his house a few moments later and two young bucks with strong backs emerged from the cab. Chiseler greeted them but did not bother to shake hands or waste any time on such pleasantries. Instead, he directed them to a gate in the driveway leading to the back of the house and toward a detached two-car garage.

They listened absently and nodded their heads. One of them went to the rear of the van and pulled the lever to lower the lift gate. I took the time to turn up the radio volume on the local news station and to hold a copy of today's LA Times in front of the camera briefly, verifying for the audience the earliest possible date my tax-cheating pal had set up his phony business.

Before long, equipment began making its way from the van, down the lift-gate, and into the garage of Mr. Chiseler. He must have fancied himself a "Man of Steel" because he obviously had chosen the "Welding Shop" option of Sid's patented "A" plan. Transported up the driveway were welding machines, grinders, oxygen and acetylene tanks, welding rod ovens, a large steel table that you could have landed an airplane on, and sheet after sheet of steel and aluminum in various cuts, gauges, and dimensions.

All of this happened under the watchful eye and nervous direction of Mr. Chiseler, who alternated between supervising the movements of the two men, and glancing up and down the street to see which one of his neighbors might be spying the action. He looked about as guilty as a whore in church, and would not do himself any favors if this tape were to make it into the hands of even the most uninspired of tax auditors.

While the camera was rolling and picking up all of the action, I used the time to work on a grocery list for my dinner with Naoko tonight. I was going to make her my trademark Chicken Marsala, along with angel-hair pasta, and steamed asparagus, and had to grab a few things from the store when I was done here.

Before the men finished or I could complete my list, my laptop pinged that a new e-mail had landed in my in-box. I switched windows and clicked on it. It had come through the "Your Secrets Are Safe" website, and by the name of the e-mail appeared to be from the woman at the Peacock. "Good," I thought. She was ready to roll over and play nice.

I couldn't have been further from the mark.

"Why do you keep doing this to me?" the e-mail demanded. "I'm already paying you money for the other tape!"

"What?" I thought to myself.

Someone was already blackmailing Marion Holtzinger!

FIVE

I went for a bike ride after finishing at Chiseler's house. Not because the weather had continued cooperating – our brief flirtation with sunshine had ended and the afternoon marine layer was already creeping in – but because I needed to sort a couple of things out.

My vehicle of choice for these head-cleaning forays was a Bianchi 928 Carbon T-Cube; A custom built, forty-thousand dollar racing bike that I had taken as payment from Mr. Dell Asplund, an aspiring cyclist with dreams of winning the Tour de France. Asplund had decided at some point in his career that he would do whatever it took to win the coveted yellow jersey, including pumping his body full of the latest performance enhancing substances. I had gotten a line on his supplier and leaned on him to forfeit his fancy wheels to me in exchange for a vow of silence regarding his deal with the Devil. He played along and then continued down the same road he was on – literally and figuratively. Banned substances or not, it still wasn't enough to carry him to the finish line ahead of the others. He slipped further in the rankings, lost his sponsors, and was unable to get picked up by even the most desperate of teams. The last I heard, he was a PE coach at a high school.

The South Bay bike path began literally outside the door of my condo in South Redondo Beach, in an area known as the "Avenues" for its alphabetical naming of the streets. I lived just off Avenue "G", and had only to roll my bike down the long ramp to the path, climb aboard, and head north toward the terminus in Pacific Palisades, twenty-two miles up the coast. I figured I would ride about half this distance to Marina del Rey, before turning back to head home.

On the way towards the Marina, I passed by the beaches of Hermosa, Manhattan, and Dockweiler. The sky had turned the color of slate and the sun's bright disc was reduced to the hue of a tarnished nickel. The water looked like mercury, and a few stubborn surfers still persisted in mastering the glass before the afternoon winds came in and sent them home.

The way I saw it, I had two issues to deal with. The first was how to handle the Chiseler's bogus tax return. One-time payments were always my preferred method of choice as they were easier to manage, and didn't require any maintenance of the account after the individual paid up. The problem in a case like this, was that Chiseler was probably already up to his eyeballs in debt, and wouldn't have the funds if I demanded a large one-time fee. In fact, I wouldn't have been surprised if he had to borrow the money from friends or family just to pay for Sid's services. He just seemed like that kind of a guy. That left easy monthly payments as my only way to reap something for my efforts.

I had already done a little quick and dirty math, and estimated what his tax obligation should have been had he been honest. I added into this the penalties and late fees, and came up with a nice large number. This, of course, did not take into account the possibility that the IRS would go after him criminally, and what grief that would have caused in his life, but I decided to just stick with the hard facts at this point, and not delve too far into speculation.

I then did a back calculation of the one-time payment, and spread it out over seven years. To this I added compound interest and something for inflation, and presto, Chiseler would find himself in just about the same financial boat he would have been in if he had just played it clean. Tough luck Mr. Chiseler.

The second issue I had to confront was more vexing and mysterious. In my fifteen years in this business, I had squeezed businessman, teachers, housewives, priests, cops, judges, professional athletes - and everything in-between. What I had never done was have a mark that someone else was already leaning on. The part of me that was all logic and business said that I should not take any of this into account, and that it shouldn't make any difference how I played it. But the gut side of me, the instinct, the curiosity, screamed for a different tack. I was missing something here, and just maybe it was opportunity knocking.

I passed under the flight path of LAX just as a jumbo jet was taking off and heading out over the Pacific. As it screamed overhead, I passed a slow moving woman on a single speed bike. I yelled, "On your left," as I blazed past and saw her twitch a little from being startled.

By the time I reached my turnaround point at the bridge crossing Ballona Creek in Playa Del Rey, the wind had begun to pick up and add a chill to the air. I got off my bike and leaned it up against the high sidewalk that ran up both sides of the bridge. A group of other cyclists had done the same and were resting their saddle-sore bums on the curb and talking. A couple of patient fishermen hunched over the side railing were keeping alive the hope that they would having something edible, if not brag-able, to show for their efforts. They spit into the water every so often as if this would draw the catch to the surface. I walked to the end of the bridge and stared out into the channel that connected the marina to the ocean.

The case of the Peacock woman had an enticing scent to it. I ran the e-mail over and over in my mind. Who was blackmailing her? How did they get wind of it? What was this "other tape" she spoke of? Was it sex...or something even worse – or better, as the case may have been?

I pondered the possibilities as a few boats idled past me in the channel. Relying on human power alone was a crew of female rowers in a powder blue boat that had "UCLA" emblazoned on its side in big yellow letters. You could just make out the call of the cadence emanating from the stern of the craft as it slipped easily through the water. Before long, I realized what I would have to do with the Peacock woman case, and got back on the Bianchi to race home and check on my hunch. I rode past the anglers just as one of them was pulling up an empty hook and cursing it for betraying him.

* * *

The wind that had come up was behind me on the return trip, and I made it back to the condo in record time. After a quick shower and shave, I trudged over to the nearby Trader Joe's to pick up some fresh sage and asparagus, as well as a bottle of Mount Eden Estates Chardonnay for Naoko.

Back home I cracked open a beer before I did anything else and took a long, thirsty pull on it.

Aggghhhh..."Mother's Milk."

I put Naoko's Chardonnay in the wine cooler, set my beer down, and began bringing out the pots, pans, utensils and other ingredients for dinner. The chicken breasts had already been split, floured and seasoned earlier, and I had only to chop the sage, sauté it for a bit in butter, and then drop in the poultry.

While the sage was cooking, I switched on my laptop. I returned to the sage just as it was getting done, stirred it a little, turned up the heat, and dropped in the four half breasts to let them cook. I filled the pot and a steamer with water for the pasta and asparagus respectively, checked on the chicken briefly, and returned to the laptop.

I fired off a terse e-mail to Hard Case letting him know I was wise to his little ruse with the obit, and that his behavior was going to result in his payments being doubled. He would whine, scream and cry foul of course, but I was used to his tantrums, and they would serve no useful purpose. He was lucky I just didn't move him into One Eyed Jack's dreaded "More trouble than you're worth" column, and fry his ass permanently by sending all the goods to his wife when she returned from her cruise. Then Hard Case would be the one going "Bon Voyage'" ...minus, of course, the "Bon" part.

I took another decent swig on my beer and returned to the frying pan to turn the chicken to cook the other side. I was flipping the last piece as my personal cell rang a familiar chime. I flipped it open and saw a text from Naoko.

It read:

"On my way. Hungry, thirsty and...;-)"

I smiled and returned to the laptop. I would have about fifteen minutes, give or take, before she got here and I wanted to check on the thing that was nagging me. I pulled up the video from the Peacock and expanded the screen to full size. I hit play and dragged the bottom scroll bar to the point where Marion Holtzinger had stood in the doorway of the motel room, and stared toward the camera.. When I found the spot I was looking for, I paused it, and returned to the kitchen.

I polished off the beer and lifted the chicken out of the pan and into a warming dish. This went into the oven to stay warm while I de-glazed the pan. In went a cup of Marsala wine followed by an equal amount of chicken broth. The pan sizzled and crackled, and the alcohol in the Marsala instantly vaporized into an aromatic cloud that could get you high if you let it. I scraped the brown bits of cooked sage and chicken off the bottom and stirred them into the sauce as it began to boil up.

When everything was sufficiently mixed, I lowered the heat to simmer and checked on the Chardonnay. It had chilled sufficiently and I uncorked it, and got out two glasses. I poured myself a glass and returned to the laptop.

Still frozen on the computer screen was Mrs. Marion Holtzinger, a.k.a. – The Peacock Woman – standing in the doorframe of the motel room just as she was about to commit the act of adultery. I had seen many videos of people in the moment of their departure from fidelity, but this one was different. I went frame by frame through the scene several times, searching. There was something different about this video, and this woman, and I needed to put my finger on it. Finally...

Bingo! There it was.

Now I knew what I had to do.

I took a slow sip on my wine – it was good – and pulled up Mrs. Holtzinger's e-mail. I typed in the instructions and sent it off, hoping I wasn't making a huge mistake. I shut down the laptop and returned to the kitchen. The sauce was looking good. I stirred it once more and heard the front door being unlocked. I poured a glass of the wine for Naoko and presented it to her with a flourish just as stepped through the door. She took a big sip and then kissed me longingly on the lips.

"Aaaaggghhh," she moaned. "Perfect timing."

"Yes," I agreed, "Perfect timing."

SIX

Venice Beach, California is where reality opted to take a decidedly different tack. Nestled snugly between the liberal enclave of Santa Monica and the pricey yacht harbors of Marina del Rey, the canal-laden Venice was part Tijuana outdoor market/part Rio Carnival/part nut-house. A "must see" destination for tourists from across the US and around the world, it laid claim to world famous Muscle Beach, chain saw jugglers, and a graffiti wall that had been sprayed on so many times through the years, the paint was now over three inches thick.

Washington Boulevard represented the southern-most boundary of the city and dead-ended at the Venice pier and a public parking lot. Numerous coffee shops and restaurants dotted either side of the street, and it was at one of these, The Grinder, that I had instructed Marion Holtzinger to meet me at eleven o'clock sharp.

Meeting a mark in person was a very risky exercise and I eschewed its practice normally. But this was an extraordinary case, and I realized that the usual methods of communication: e-mails, phone calls, anonymous correspondence, wouldn't suffice for my purposes, and so I decided to take the chance. There were always ways to mitigate the risk involved.

I had arrived a half-hour earlier and stationed myself a short distance out on the Venice Pier. Surfers shredded the waves in the water below me, and a John Deere tractor chugged across the beach, it's exhaust stack billowing black smoke as it dredged the sand for trash. A deranged homeless man with an overflowing shopping cart was sprawled out on the concrete a few feet away from me, delivering an impassioned soliloquy, and solving all of the problems of the world except his own. In all, it was just one more crazy day, in a crazy city, at the edge of the world.

I spotted Holtzinger's familiar silver Camry as it pulled into the parking lot at the foot of the pier at five minutes to eleven. She received her ticket, parked, exited her vehicle, and strode purposefully toward Washington Boulevard and The Grinder. I kept an eye out for other cars that might have followed her and found none. I also didn't spot her making any gestures, or knowing nods, to other vehicles or characters that might have arrived before her.

She took a seat at The Grinder at an outdoor table facing west as I had instructed. I dropped two quarters into the pay telescope on the pier and watched the magnified scene in the viewfinder as the unit clicked to life.

The sound of the coins dropping into the machine triggered a Pavlonian-type response from the homeless man at my feet.

"Hey buddy, do you have any extra change you could spare?"

"Later," I replied absently, and he went back to his sad monologue. I removed my sunglasses and popped my eye-patch over my empty left eye socket; it was the only way I would be able to see through the scope.

She was dressed in a smart business suit the color of washed sand. Her blouse was modestly cut, snow white, and had a minor strip of ruffles running along the bodice. Her shoes were closed toe pumps with two inch heels. They were the same color as her suit and she sat with her knees together facing me. Her legs were nice.

A few moments after she took her seat, a waiter appeared and handed her a note. She read it, frowned, and then sighed before reaching into her purse to retrieve her cell phone. My earpiece chimed a few seconds later. I answered it without taking my eyes off her.

"Go to the restaurant across the street, Cucina Pazzo," I said. "Take a table on the outdoor patio. Face north. I'll be there in a few minutes."

"I don't like –," she started to answer before I cut her off.

"Do it," I said firmly. "...Or I start mailing DVDs."

I hung up on her without waiting for a retort.

She stared at the phone's display for a long moment before finally snapping it shut. She dropped it back into her purse, stood up, and headed across the street to the restaurant. I studied her the whole time. She didn't make another call, or look out to any hidden accomplice to let them know the venue had changed. I was beginning to feel that she was playing it nice. Just to be sure though, I made one final sweep of the street with the telescope. I didn't see her beau "Tough Guy", and nobody else out there looked like a cop, a leg-breaker, the Pope, or James Bond. I swung the telescope away, pulled off my patch, and replaced my sunglasses.

"Hey buddy," Mister Homeless asked. "How'd you lose your eye?"

"Pan-handling," I said, and began walking toward the restaurant.

Just as I reached the foot of the pier and was crossing the bike path, two identical twin girls about seven years old, wearing identical pink outfits, and on identical pink bikes, came out of nowhere and nearly hit me. In reality, it wasn't out of nowhere, but out of the area of peripheral vision that I no longer enjoyed, due to my missing ocular.

"Watch out!" their father yelled, although I wasn't sure whether the comment was directed to them or to me.

The Cucina Pazzo was a funky little Italian restaurant with great food at great prices. More importantly to me was the fact that the building itself had been through so many evolutions of remodel and combining with other buildings, that it's layout resembled a confusing labyrinth of short halls, dead ends, and unmarked exits that led out to the back-streets and alleys of Venice. It was The Winchester Mystery House of restaurants. I had parked the Mini-Van a few blocks away, and had a bike stashed in the alley just outside the restaurant. I purposely told Marion Holtzinger to take a seat facing north. Sitting opposite her, I could keep watch for any potential threats that came through the patio's arched entrance. If things got dicey, I could make a quick dash into the building, through the maze, out one of the many exits and onto my bike faster than Keye's mouse Algernon.

The lunch crowd had yet to materialize and the patio was deserted when I walked in. I sat down at her table and, skipping any small talk or pleasantries, gave her a stern warning.

"If you've contacted the police or had anybody come with you, I'll get up, walk away, and have the video of you and your boyfriend on the Internet by the end of the day. Do you understand?"

She stared at me for a long moment. "I've contacted no one. I just want this over."

I nodded. I felt like she was telling the truth. I had a better look at her now. She was thinner than she looked on the video and had a lean, worried face. I wondered how much of it might have been due to recent events. Her hair was the same as I remembered it; blond, well coifed and with some streaks of gray here and there. She had on a pair of sunglasses so I couldn't see her eyes, but the beginnings of some crows-feet sprouted from the corners. Her nose was slightly turned up at the tip.

She wore small diamond stud earrings and had her wedding ring on. Other than that, she had no other jewelry. She was an attractive woman from a distance, and she still was up close.

"Okay," I said. "First off, I'm not the one who's been blackmailing you."

She didn't jump for joy and yell, "Yippee!" but I didn't expect her to either. Instead, she shook her head, confused.

"I...I don't get it. Aren't you the one who left the DVD on my car? Didn't you e-mail me to meet you here?"

"Yes. But I've never contacted you before Tuesday. You mentioned in your e-mail about another tape and about wanting me to leave you alone. I'd like to find out what this is all about and who else is leaning on you."

She was stunned; what were the chances?

"I can't believe it," she said, shaking her head in disgust. "You mean I've got not one, but *two* assholes blackmailing me?"

Her voice was beginning to rise and I didn't like it. Thankfully, the waiter arrived a moment later and went through his usual drill. He left two water glasses and menus. She didn't bother to pick hers up.

"I don't want anything," she said narrowly.

"It's on me," I said as I scanned my menu. "Go ahead and get what you want."

She made a slight snorting sound as if to mock my thin sliver of graciousness. I didn't care; I was hungry and was going to eat.

When the waiter returned a few minutes later, she had acquiesced and decided to get a salad and a Diet Coke. I don't think she felt like eating, but might have figured that food would be a good stalling technique if she wanted time to formulate answers to my questions. I settled on a ham and cheese Panini and iced tea.

When he departed to place our orders, I steered us back to the topic at hand.

"So anyway, I want to find out more about this other person: What's he, or she - or them, got on you? How long has it been going on...the whole bit."

"Why is that any of your concern?" She as much snipped as said.

She was feistier than I had expected.

"Maybe I don't like any competition," I shot back, hearing my own voice rise a bit. "Maybe because the more someone else gets from you, the less you can pay me. Maybe because I'm a copy-cat and I want to study his brush-strokes...and maybe because I think there's a lot more going on here than meets the eye."

The last statement got her attention, as I had intended. She stiffened ever so slightly and her breath caught in her throat. She tried hard to retain her composure and not appear rattled. It didn't work.

"Wh – what do you mean by that?"

"I mean that Bozo you were with; Bill Batty. He's a crude, rude dude – a buffoon. You're an attractive woman. If you were looking to get laid - why with a clown like him? Hell, you could probably even get yourself a little boy-toy if you were so persuaded"

"Will you please stop talking like that; it's sordid.'

"I'll knock it off when I get some answers."

From across the patio a man called out.

"Jack!"

I turned toward the voice as he approached our table. It was the owner of the Cucina Pazzo. He reached our table and pumped my hand vigorously.

"Good to see you again Jack. Is everything okay? Can I get you anything?"

I smiled back at him.

"We're fine," I said and released his hand.

"Ok," he said. You let me know if there's anything you need."

"Will do," I said and he disappeared back into the kitchen.

"So your name is Jack?" Marion Holtzinger said.

"That's what people call me."

"But is that your name?"

"That's what people call me," I repeated, realizing she was trying to change the topic. "So let's get back to this other blackmailer...and to you doing the horizontal slam-dance with Bill Batty. Why don't you tell me what's going on."

She stared at me for a long while, silently. I could tell she was trying to figure out how to respond. Finally...

"And how do you know that I don't like him?" she challenged. "Maybe he really turns me on. Maybe he's great in bed. And what business is it of yours what my taste in men is? As long as you get your money; you shouldn't give a hoot."

"That's true," I admitted. "But like I said; I think there's a lot more going on here - and I want to know about it. I don't believe for a second that you have any desires for him. Disgust was written all over your face the moment before you stepped into the motel room at The Peacock. Why do you have to sleep with him Marion? What does he have on you?"

She was saved for the time being as the waiter arrived with our food. We were both quiet and pleasant as he set out our modest presentation. We began to eat. The silence persisted with a slow tension building between us. Finally, she broke it.

"You don't even know me, Jack – or whatever the heck your name is. How can you be so sure I don't want anything to do with Bill? Just because of a 'look' you say I gave? You can tell all of that from just a split second on a video?"

I set my fork down and took a sip of iced tea.

"I can tell because I'm an expert, Marion – plan and simple. An expert in an occupation that granted, at its most generous description, is a dubious one, and at its worst – a parasite. But I do it well and I know people. I know how to predict their behavior, and most importantly, I know how to read them. I wouldn't have survived this long if I couldn't. And yes, I could tell just by the look you gave on the video, that you no more wanted to be with that oaf than you wanted to have a root canal. Your eyes said it all."

She put her head down slightly, touched a finger to her sunglasses to adjust them up. She probably wasn't even aware she was doing it.

"I know something is going on Marion. And I think that this other blackmailer might be the key."

She picked at her salad and took a small sip from her Diet Coke, avoiding my stare. I noticed her hand was trembling slightly. The only sounds on the patio were the trickling of water in the faux Venetian fountains and of the few birds that flitted about chirping playfully. I waited.

"You could tell all of that just from the video?" she finally asked.

I nodded. "Like I said; 'I'm an expert.'"

I could tell that she was impressed with my skill-set, but she wasn't about to give me any credit. That was ok; I was used to it. She pondered the situation for a long time. After a moment, she looked around the empty patio and then leaned a little closer toward me.

"If I tell you all about this other blackmailer, do you think you can find him?"

"Him, her, or them," I corrected. "Yes. I probably can."

"Can you get rid of him for me?"

I gave her a level stare. "If you mean 'get rid of' as in kill - no, I don't do murder. If you mean 'get them off your back,' then it's a possibility. I'm good at finding people, but getting them to lay off you may not be so simple. It might be a lot of work – and dangerous. Besides getting rid of a little bit of competition; what's in it for me?"

Now it was her turn to stare back at me. She set her fork down gently next to her salad plate. She set her elbows down on the table and slowly laced her hands in front of her. Her wedding ring glinted in the sunlight. She stared right at me.

"You're in the business of dirty little secrets aren't you?" she said.

I nodded slowly.

"I have a good one for you."

SEVEN

A brief lesson here, Dear Reader, on the study of Secrets 101. There are secrets in this world...and then, there are *secrets*. All have some degree of value — both perceived and potential — but how much they are truly worth is based upon several factors.

The first of these has to do with the relationship of the secret, relative to the position of the person, persons, organization, or government privy to - or affected by it. For example, the stolen plans to a US missile defense system could be worth millions of dollars to the Russian or Chinese military, but virtually worthless to the Afghan goat herder eking out a living for his family.

Conversely, the military leadership of these countries would have no interest in the fact that the goat herder is surreptitiously grazing his herd on his neighbor's land, but the herder would be terrified by the fact that he might have his hands cut off if discovered. This is in essence, the yin and yang of secrets.

The second factor has to do with the resources a person, organization, or country has for keeping secrets under wraps. Although the ramifications of exposure run the gamut from simple embarrassment, to the loss of a job, divorce, jail time - or in extreme cases, death - if the affected party doesn't have the means to contain the information from public view, the secret, however juicy, becomes worthless. In all my years of doing this, I can never remember blackmailing a homeless man. While she may have thought it valuable, Marion Holtzinger's secret could run anywhere within this vast range of possibilities.

"Exactly what are we talking about here?" I prodded.

"I told you; a dirty little secret."

"How much money is involved?"

"Hundreds of thousands, possibly millions."

"Person or persons?"

"Persons...a business."

"Corporation?"

"Limited partnership."

"You have solid information?"

"Yes. As the saying goes; I know where all the 'bodies are buried' - figuratively speaking of course."

I took another bite of my Panini and pondered what she had said. Marion waited patiently. I didn't think she was bluffing. My hunch that there was something more going on here than your typical boff-fest was correct; but it was going to get complicated, messy - possibly even dangerous - before it was over.

"And you'll tell me all about this 'dirty little secret' involving possibly millions of dollars if I locate the other person who's blackmailing you?"

She nodded.

"Yes," she said. "Find them and stop them."

"What about Bill?"

"What about him?"

"Are they blackmailing him too?"

"Yes. He told me he received a similar letter in the mail a couple of days before I did. He called and warned me to be on the lookout for it. He said he'd love to find whoever's doing this and kill them"

"I'm sure he would. Did you tell him you were meeting with me today?"

"No."

"Good. Keep it that way. When I find these guys, don't tell him about it. He can keep paying them for all I care. You're the one bringing something to the table. Do you understand?"

She nodded.

"Like I said; finding them won't be that hard, but I can't guarantee that I can stop them."

She picked up her fork and took another bite of her salad.

"Why not? I mean if you know who they are; can't you get the "goods" if you will, from them?"

As she said this, she held up her two hands and made a gesture of quotation marks with her fingers.

"And besides that, aren't you the expert?" she mocked. "Didn't you just spend the last couple of minutes telling me how great you were?"

I finished the last bite of my sandwich and wiped the napkin across my mouth. I didn't like her tone. It was condescending and sarcastic. She felt that she had a little bargaining power now and it was going to her head. Before long, she would start trying to dictate terms to me. I decided to set the tone for the rest of this meeting. I reached into my back pocket and pulled out a couple sheets of paper stapled together. I unfolded them and tossed them across the table at her. It was a copy of all of the contacts in her Yahoo e-mail account, as well as the password to it.

"Alright listen here," I said. "You don't like me; I understand that. But you're going to work with me or else everyone on that list is going to get a nice attachment from you in their in-box. Got it?"

She read down the list and her face went pale. After a few moments, I reached back for the papers. Her hand was shaking so badly the sheets made a fluttering sound. I refolded them and set them on the table.

"So, to answer your question about me stopping them by getting 'the goods' - meaning the tape you referred to when you first responded to me – is not going to be as easy as you think. First of all, you say 'tape,' as in the singular. They would have multiple copies if they were smart. And, this is the computer age. The old days of a couple of black and white photos taped under a toilet tank lid, or in a safe, are long gone. They would have burned several DVDs, put copies on flash-drives, mailed a download of it to themselves at various e-mail accounts – it could be anywhere out on the cloud. In short, even if I was able to find and destroy ten copies - which wouldn't be that easy - they could still have a hundred more out there. You'd never be able to sleep at night for the rest of your life wondering when the shoe was going to drop."

She snorted, "You think I sleep now?"

I let it go and she was quiet for a moment, digesting what I had said.

"So it's hopeless then?" she said finally. "No matter what I give you, I'll never be able to get them off my back."

"I didn't say it was hopeless – only difficult. There's only two ways to stop them – and one I told you I wouldn't do. And even if I was of that ilk, murder still wouldn't end your problems – it would only be the beginning."

"Why is that?" she asked innocently enough that I knew she wasn't being disingenuous.

"First of all, you have to get away with it. Murder is not as easy as the TV and movies would have you believe. The first thing they would do is to look into this person's effects and find the tape of you and Bill...probably along with several others. You'd be a suspect because you had a motive for seeing this person dead. You'd be dragged in, a million questions would be asked, and they would break you. Even if you could bluff your way through it and pull it off, there's still the poison pill aspect of offing them."

"Poison pill?"

"The Internet – remember. All sorts of things that we could never imagine it being used for: Facebook, Youtube, eBay, and so on. So, several enterprising entrepreneurs have come up with sites like Life-Switch."

"Life-Switch?"

I nodded. "It's a site for people to give their final instructions, or say goodbye to friends and family if they die suddenly. You can add in all sorts of attachments: wills, burial instructions, videos of you saying goodbye to people – that sort of thing. You have a pre-determined e-mail contact list, and they set up a prompt for you on a regular basis. If you don't reply to the prompt after a certain number of tries, the site automatically figures that you have met your demise, and sends out the attachments to your contact list."

I made a slight gesture toward her contact list on the table.

"And that contact list could be yours Mrs. Holtzinger... and the attachment could be the tape of you and Bill."

She sighed wearily and put her face into her hands, her head shaking from side to side.

"How did things ever get so complicated?" she said to no one and to everyone.

The waiter came by and took our plates. I offered up the idea of coffee. Surprisingly, she accepted.

"What's 'the other way' you mentioned?" she said through her hands.

"We'll cross that bridge if we come to it," I told her. "For now; let's just concentrate on finding them."

"Ok," she said, nodding.

* * *

For the next half-hour or so, I debriefed her on the particulars of the other extortion plot against her: When did she start her affair with Bill? What motel was the other video shot at? How much were they squeezing her for? How did they communicate with her?

In the meantime, the lunch crowd was beginning to arrive and take up spots around us. Several times we had to stop talking and our tone dropped to conspiratorial tones. In all, Marion Holtzinger was very forthcoming and laid it out in tidy chronological order. The only sticking point came when I asked her to give me a copy of the video of her and Bill. Unlike my DVD, this had been shot through the window of the hotel where a tryst had occurred, and showed the two of them engaged in carnal activity. It took some doing to break down her modesty, but I finally convinced her that the video might be the most important piece of the puzzle to help me find - and hopefully – stop them.

"When do you have to make the next payment?" I asked.

"I just sent it yesterday," she said." To the PO Box I told you about."

"Ok," I said." I think that's all I need for now. I'll be in touch."

I stood up. "Let's go."

We started to stand up to leave, and then she stopped suddenly. "What about the check?" she asked.

"Don't worry about it." I said.

I didn't tell her that all of the remodeling done on the Cucina Pazzo had never been permitted.

EIGHT

I had two stops to make after leaving Marion Holtzinger. One was the motel where the tape had been shot. The other, was the El Segundo Post Office where her payments were being sent. How does one blackmailer find another blackmailer? He tries to retrace their steps.

The motel was located just north of the Los Angeles International Airport and was the closer of the two. It was named "Airport Inn," and was located on a side street off of Sepulveda Boulevard. Before leaving Venice, I checked out the address on Google Earth. As seen from space, it appeared as a small "L" shape structure that was abutted on three sides by other buildings. I could see a narrow access at the rear and along one side of the motel. Marion had told me that the video of her and Bill had been shot through the window from the outside of the middle room on the long side of the "L." If anyone were going to shoot video into a room, it would be from here.

My observations of the layout were confirmed when I arrived a few minutes later and found the Airport Inn nestled snugly between the cut-rate filling station, the back end of an auto repair facility, and a large two-story apartment building. The short side of the "L" contained three of the motel's ten rooms. The long side ran perpendicular toward the side-street, and was anchored by what I figured was the registration office. The inn looked shabby from the outside with peeling paint and a roof that could probably hold back as much water as a fisherman's net, but that didn't stop it from proudly advertising the fact that it was, 'Airport close' and had free WI-Fi in the rooms. Three cars were in the parking lot with their owners apparently inside the rooms doing God knows what. It looked like just one more place where people could fulfill whatever fantasies their wallets and their conscience could afford. A neon sign, barely visible in the bright sunshine, offered vacancy.

I parked at the back of the gas station lot and reached into the center console for my digital camera. Jets from the airport were taking off and landing every few minutes and the glass on the mini-van vibrated as the engines spun up. I snapped several stills of the building: wide angle, a close-up of the registration office, and several close-ups of the rooms. I had the video camera in the van, but I didn't see the need for any tape at the moment.

I tucked the camera into my pocket and strode toward the Airport Inn. A weed infested stone planter in the rough shape of a half circle and with a few missing stones abutted the front of the registration office. One forlorn stone lay on the cracked pavement where gravity had taken it and no one had bothered to pick it up. Within the compromised rampart, a single valiant tree leaned precariously toward the street and refused to die in spite of the neglect it endured.

I stepped inside the office and it was like a million other sleazy motels I had been in over the years. The room was small and stuffy, and the sickening sweet smell of incense throttled your nostrils before you were even fully inside. A registration counter topped with a Formica surface that had gone out of style in the fifties stood opposite the door. A couple of cheap Naugahyde chairs sat on an opposite wall and were separated by a mismatched table containing several dog-eared and torn magazines that were at least five years old. The Airport Inn had all the charm and ambience of a bus station. I made my way over to the counter and lightly pressed the bell to summon some assistance. The bell was sticky and my hand felt like it had touched a half-finished lollipop.

Beckoned by the promise of another booking, a hopeful looking Pakistani man in a mauve turban and dressed in a purple shirt and beige and brown stripped pants, pushed through a stained velvet curtain that separated the office from another room. He smelled of curry and too much deodorant. I caught a brief glance of a small living room with an older TV and a fabric-covered sofa that looked like it had been used for target practice. A middle-aged woman, I guessed to be the man's wife, dressed in a brightly colored sari, sat on the sofa watching cartoons.

"Yes my friend," the man beamed. "How can I help you?"

"How much are your rooms?" I asked.

"By the hour or the day?" he smiled.

Before I could begin to answer, another plane throttled its jet engines up for takeoff and I had to pause a few moments until the din passed. The Pakistani just looked at me and smiled.

"By the day," I said when the sound had died out sufficiently.

"Seventy eight dollars a day."

"Do you take dogs?" I asked.

"I am sorry sir," he said apologetically. "We cannot."

I nodded my understanding; PETA would probably protest the mistreatment of animals.

"Ok. Thanks."

I turned away, my hand sticking to the knob as I pulled open the door.

I stepped outside and before anything else, took a breath of fresh air. A screaming jet lined up on final approach in the distance. I pulled out my cell and made a sham of making a call. After a few seconds, I nonchalantly turned toward the registration office. The proprietor had ducked back into his living room to finish watching TV. It was probably getting close to the good part and he didn't want to miss it.

I strode back over to the gas station and made a sharp left turn when I stepped onto the lot. I walked to the far northern end and then crossed back over a low cinder block wall onto the motel property and towards the short end of the "L." I set my cell to silent, stepped behind the building and crept along the backside of the rooms. The area was about five feet wide and had been paved with fresh asphalt during the Eisenhower administration. Cracks were abundant and weeds and crabgrass pushed through unmolested. The auto repair facility that bordered the rear of the Airport Inn had a white stucco wall that was at least fifteen feet high and contained no windows. Enough graffiti was present on the walls to assure me that it was easy enough to prowl around back here and get away with it. Inside one of the rooms, a thumping headboard beat out a cadence of lust in "two-two" time. Someone was getting his or her money's worth.

I reached the intersection of the long side of the building and this was where the terrain changed. Somewhere during the course of time, a patch of ivy had taken over and carpeted the ground beneath me. To my left was the backside of the remaining rooms, one of which, according to Marion, had been used as the set for the Holtzinger/Batty show. To my right was the backside of a two-story apartment building. This section would be a little bit trickier.

I began stepping through the ivy towards the front of the building in an effort to get closer to Room 4 and check out the set-up. It was slow going. The ivy was dry and brittle and it cracked noisily under my feet. I could hear a vacuum cleaner running in one of the apartments, and a baby was screaming at the top of its lungs and trying to compete with the jets. I hoped the sound of the planes would mask my own footfalls as I tried to coordinate my steps with the takeoffs and landings.

As I moved along, I checked out the construction of the motel windows. They were old single-pane aluminum sliders. Through the dirty glass, I could see the plastic backing of the cheap draperies that hung in the room. Security was handled by the installation of some of those flimsy window clamps that were supposed to keep outsiders from getting in. They were probably one of the first things a neophyte burglar learned to compromise.

A new flight revved up for take up in the distance and I moved forward. I was about halfway toward my goal of Room 4 when I heard a window screech open over my right shoulder.

"Hey asshole!" a male voice called out angrily.

I turned toward the sound and saw a young man in his mid to late twenties glaring at me through the opened window of one of the apartments. The window screen had pulled out from one of the corners of its frame and it waved lazily like a flag on a summer day. The man was dressed in a wife-beater shirt and had bulging arms covered in angry tattoos. He held an opened can of Budweiser in one of his hands.

"What the fuck are you doing back here?" he demanded.

"I thought my cat went back here." I said, appealing to his gentler side...of which none was in residence.

"Well it's not back here! So get the fuck out before I come out there and light your fuckin' ass up!"

"No problem," I said easily and then turned to walk back. "I'm sure Fluffy will find her way home."

He glared at me the whole time as I walked past, his eyes never leaving me as he took a swig of beer from the can. When I was sufficiently out of range to be a threat, he slammed the window closed with a screech while muttering "mother fucking cat!" under his breath. That was it, as far as the Airport Inn went.

* * *

I received a much warmer reception at the El Segundo Post Office. I maintained a PO Box here and knew the layout of the place fairly well... just not from a stakeout perspective. I strolled in just like one more customer on an average day. Marion sent her payments to Box 214. The one I maintained was 263. I spied 214 and stood in front of it, gauging an angle through the large plate glass window that ran across the side of the building. My car was parked on the street just on the other side of this wall. I couldn't see it from where I stood at the box, but if the car in front of me moved and I pulled forward, I would have a good shot of it.

I pulled a pad of Post-it-Notes from my pocket and scrawled a quick message on the top paper.

"Lou – give me a call. Sam"

I stuck the note onto Box 213, just above my target, and then moved on to my own box. Two envelopes were inside, both from the re-mailing

71

service, so I knew that the eagle had landed once again. I closed the box and headed back out to the mini-van to wait to move up.

While I was waiting in the van, I went through the envelopes. The first was a monthly payment from a crooked dentist office that was double billing Medicare against its patients. I had cozied up to an embittered ex-employee who had thankfully kept a CD of all the shenanigans that had transpired over the last several years. I purchased the CD from her outright for a thousand dollars when she couldn't afford to make her rent. So far, it had netted me over three thousand in monthly payments.

The second envelope was from a dirt-bag biker who had been involved in a scam involving welding new serial plates onto stolen Harleys. He was a charming fellow who had promised a death by draw-and-quartering if he ever found me.

Guess what Dirt-Bag; you never will.

Besides the bike scam he was running, he also abandoned his family and left his wife destitute with three kids to raise. All of his income, even his legitimate work, was under the table so the courts were hamstrung trying to get him to cough up his child support.

I reached behind the seat and grabbed a portable file box that contained an assortment of envelopes, notepads, rubber bands, postage stamps, and other office supplies. I filled out the front of the envelope with the name and address of Dirt-Bag's ex-wife, folded a dark piece of paper over the cash, and placed it into the envelope. As soon as the car ahead of me moved and I pulled into its place, I could go inside and mail the envelope to her. The poor wife never knew about her husband's scam or my squeeze on him, and the only thing I ever asked her to do was to never say a word to him or to try to find me. She referred to me as her Knight in Shining Armor.

A woman with a young child in tow passed by the van and clicked a key-fob to get into the car ahead of me. It took her a while to get the kid settled in his car seat and finally pull away, but when she did, I started the mini-van and idled up slowly, my eyes looking toward the plate glass window and the boxes inside. The one with the Post-it-Note on it came into view and I moved forward a few more feet to center it in the frame of the window. I would have the video camera mounted in the middle seat area and so I climbed back there to take a look.

Good work One Eyed Jack; I had a clean shot of the box and could get the whole thing on tape as soon as anyone came to collect their prize. Done with that.

I got out of the van with the envelope to go inside to mail it, and multi-tasked by calling a cab company at the same time. I gave them the address of the post office and they said they could have a car there in less than ten minutes. I flipped the phone closed, dropped the envelope with the cash into the outgoing mail slot, and returned to the van.

I didn't want to lose my perfect parking space, but I also didn't like to leave my gear in the vehicle overnight. So I got out my cameras, laptop, GPS unit, and everything else that might score another round of dope for an addict and packed them into a backpack. I only had to wait a few more minutes before the cab pulled up and took me home to my condo in Redondo Beach.

* * *

I had promised Naoko that I would make dinner for her tonight, but by the time I got dropped off and settled, that plan began to look iffy. I checked my meager larder and it didn't look promising. I knew that I could head out to the store and grab some stuff to cook up, but I would be cutting it too close and had a lot to do to prepare for tomorrow. I sent her a text explaining that I was swamped tonight and that we had to reschedule dinner.

I made a couple of PB&Js and put them into my insulated lunch box. To this I also added some water, fruit, and trail-mix, and placed the whole affair into the refrigerator where I would collect it before leaving in the morning for my stakeout. An old mayonnaise jar would serve as my portable john for the inevitable bodily functions that would arise and I would be set for a long day of staking out Box 214.

After satisfying myself that I had gotten everything ready for tomorrow, I turned my attention to the computer. I went to a new e-mail account I had instructed Marion to use and was pleased to see that she had not gotten cold feet, and had forwarded me a copy of the video clip sent to her by the other blackmailer. That was encouraging, as I had given her about a fifty-fifty chance of following through on her promise. I created a new folder titled "The Odd Couple", saved it to the aforementioned, and then opened it to play.

Before you think, Dear Reader, that I get my jollies from playing the voyeur and watching tapes of ordinary folks engaged in carnal acts, think again. Compared to mainstream pornography, un-choreographed amateur sex scenes were generally clumsy, mistimed, and dull. Add to this the typically poor lighting and frozen camera angle of a video shot strictly for extortion purposes, and you don't have much titillation to get your motor running.

The Holtzinger/Batty clip was no different. It was shot as Marion had said, through the window of the Airport Inn. Just enough of a gap between the drapes existed to reveal the bed and its occupants on the tape. Marion lay on her back with Bill on top of her, vigorously and breathlessly thrusting away in the classic missionary style. Her face was plainly visible and as I expected to see, there was no joy or lust in her eyes as she lay there listlessly.

When I replayed it the second time, I turned up the volume, but what sound there might have been, was blocked by the closed window, or masked by background noises. The correct date and time was visible in the lower half of the frame, as I thought they might have been. Not that this could actually prove a specific time something had occurred, but its existence always lent a rather official look to the product. Whoever did this was paying attention to details.

Based upon the difficulty I had encountered trying to get close to the room to re-simulate the shot, I began to suspect that it could have been more of an inside job. The camera could have been set up by opening the window from the inside of the room, placing it on a tripod outside, and then turning it on remotely. Not a great technical challenge, but this meant someone had access to the room before and after the tryst. In my years in the business, I'd seen a couple of motel managers or employees pull this sort of stunt to extort money out of the clientele, but the owner of the Airport Inn didn't strike me as such a fellow. He had a cash cow by letting people get their jollies with full immunity, and this sort of stunt would drive customers away and sully his impeccable reputation.

I replayed it four times looking for any clues the blackmailer might have left, but found none. The video was just under two minutes long, the whole encounter probably no more than an hour. In the big scheme of things, this was a miniscule amount of time in a person's life. Yet these were the moments that could change that life, the moments where lust, or greed, or arrogance trumped common sense and reasoning. Embarrassing vignettes that the extortionist hoped to capture. They were his stock and trade, and the arrows in his quiver. These were the moments that could destroy otherwise innocent lives forever. Lives just like Marion Holtzinger's.

NINE

It was the kind of day in Southern California that made mid-westerners throw down their snow shovels and move here. A robin's egg sky with just a few feathery clouds opened up a vista that stretched over eighty miles from end to end. From the balcony of my condo in Redondo Beach I could see the isthmus of Catalina Island to the south, and all the way to Point Dume in the north. Today would be a day when everyone would have a smile on their face and feel good to be alive. Angelinos would say hello to each other as they passed on the street, and a cop just might let you slide on that moving violation. Today would be a great day for a bike ride, a picnic, or to hold the end of a kite string in your hand. It would NOT be a great day to sit in a cramped car watching a PO Box that might be visited today, tomorrow, next week...or never.

My day began like the rest of the working stiffs of the world on a Thursday morning at five a.m. I showered, shaved, and ate a light breakfast. I looked at my personal cell phone for any new messages and found none. Naoko had responded to my dinner cancellation with a terse text, "Thanks for the notice!" and had not called or sent any others during the night. I read her reply at least four times and knew I was in the doghouse...again.

I had a cab pick me up at seven and we drove north towards El Segundo along the coast route. It would start warming up soon, and with it the beach traffic would thicken to the point where you began to question your sanity. I arrived at the Post Office around seven-thirty and was pleased to find that the mini-van hadn't been towed, broken into, or homesteaded by a band of gypsies. My day was shaping up.

The building wasn't set to open for another half-hour so I had plenty of time to get my equipment transferred and set up without drawing the suspicions of any on-lookers. Once I had it in place, I took advantage of the final ten minutes to walk a block over to a gas station to take my last civilized bathroom break of the day.

As a person who's trade requires the surveillance of people and capture of evidence, I have plenty of painful experience in the practice of protracted stakeouts. It didn't take long to learn all of the tricks and shortcuts to get through the days, or sometimes weeks, of patient waiting in a parked vehicle or the window of a hotel. Minutes seem like hours and days became an eternity. To get through it with all of your marbles, you first had to mitigate any and all of the physical discomforts that are bound to arise. A bathroom is a luxury that you would only be allowed at the beginning and end of your day, and so you had better take full advantage of it when you could. Hot food is another rare treat that you'd better enjoy if the option presents itself. Find some good radio programs to listen to and you're all set...at least for the first hour or two.

When I returned to the van the usual line of people had already formed outside the Post Office waiting for the doors to swing open. I climbed into the middle seat, powered up the camera and my laptop, and focused in on Box 214. I noted that the Post-it-Note was still stuck onto the box above it, but how long this would last, I couldn't say. Using a special video program I had installed on the laptop, I placed a reverse optical iris over Box 214 that would slightly darken and therefore target the area around the box on my screen, while still keeping the outer perimeter at its normal level of brightness. As soon as someone opened the box, I would have it all on tape and be ready to swing into action. Just when this would all happen was another matter.

Day One - 09:53 AM

As I had anticipated, the Post Office saw its share of waves of customers. After the initial rush, a lag ensued that lasted for ten minutes or so. Then another wave of people came, and then another lull. In just under two hours, only half a dozen people came by the mailboxes. Some stopped short before reaching the targeted box, some went past it, and one woman pulled something from Box 221, directly next to the blackmailer's box. The benchmark Post-it-Note on Box 213 had survived so far.

I took advantage of the time by catching up on some work. I moved the video capture of the box into the corner of the screen so that I could keep tabs on it, then took care of some administrative duties on the computer. I opened some new e-mail accounts and closed others, informing the appropriate marks of the changes. I caught up on the spreadsheet I used for keeping track of everything and everyone. And then, I logged into my investment account and moved some more money into my IRA. Hey, I want to retire someday too.

Day One – 12:11 PM

The lunch crowd was in full swing now and the Post Office was doing a land-office business: Mail was being dropped off and picked up, parcels were being weighed and shipped, and PO Boxes were being checked. At one point, I had two people right near Box 214 and blocking my view. I was afraid I wouldn't see it, or the person, if someone opened it, but in the end it remained untouched. The owner of Box 213 came by and saw my Post-it-Note stuck onto his box. He was a big, dumpy guy in his thirties, dressed in faded jeans and a dirty short sleeved shirt. He pulled the note off, looked at it and then crumpled it up and dropped it on the floor. He removed what looked like a box of checks and then closed and locked the door. Besides learning some good manners, he needed a shave as well.

I had finished with all of my work around eleven-thirty or so, expanded the video stream back to full screen, and turned the radio to a talk show that I really wasn't listening to. I wasn't doing much, but I was doing a lot of thinking, about yesterday. About the odds of this panning out into something profitable, and about Marion Holtzinger.

When I started out in this business, 15 years ago, most people didn't have e-mail accounts and weren't as connected to the web as they are now. The Internet had made us anonymous friends with millions of people, whether we wanted it to or not. In the old days, I had a lot more contact with my marks. It was more dangerous, but more exciting and intimate at the same time. I got to see them up close and personal. They existed before me in three dimensions as opposed to only two. I smelled their sweat as I laid their dark secrets naked before them. I felt their heated breath as they lambasted me for being a sneak and a coward, and someone who should mind their own business. I saw the tears that ran down their faces and I heard their sobs. They were real people: living, breathing, loving, and hating. Something had been lost over the past several years. I was insulated. Marks were an e-mail address and an Excel sheet entry in an ether-world. Their images were pixels on a flat screen. I know that I controlled people, manipulated them to serve my monetary needs, but the puppet strings were invisible bits of data flying across the web at the speed of light, the actions were implied. I said for them to do "A" and they did "A." At what cost of pain, or sorrow, or anguish, I never really saw or knew.

Seeing Marion up close brought back all the good of it...and the bad. She wasn't a virtual stranger any longer. She was real and animated. She had emotions I could see, hear, and feel: her helplessness in this whole business, her dreams that could die hard by the hand of strangers, her life flipped topsy-turvy by happenstance and a brief lapse of judgment. I smelled her perfume and saw the softness of her skin. She was real: flesh and blood, bone and sinew. Sitting just across a table from her and sharing a meal, I had become a part of her life, and her, part of mine. I knew I shouldn't, but I pitied her for her predicament. Maybe that was why I stayed detached from my marks, why I needed to —

A body moved into the screen, blocking Box 214. He was male, small stature, and appeared young from the back. A video buffer was running that dropped out anything older than one minute. I turned the buffer off and began recording. I couldn't tell for sure if he was opening the box, but the angle and height of his arms made it appear likely. An envelope appeared in his right hand and went into his right pocket. He stepped just slightly to the side as he closed and locked the box door; it was 214.

TEN

I disconnected the camera from the laptop and quickly jumped forward into the front seat, carrying the computer with me. I set it down on the passenger's seat and connected another cable that ran from a dash mounted bullet camera to the computer's port. I started the van, idled forward slowly, so that I was closer to the entrance, and waited for him to emerge. I couldn't believe my good fortune. Naoko just may get a nice meal out of me tonight.

He came out just a few seconds later and walked unhurriedly across the street towards a battered yellow mini pick-up truck. He looked to be in his early to mid-twenties, had shoulder length brown hair, and was dressed in faded black cargo shorts and a red t-shirt. The thin wires from an iPod ran up to ear-buds under his bushy hair, and I recognized him immediately for what he was; a runner. The blackmailer wasn't using a re-mailing service to forward payments, but they weren't crazy enough to pick up the goods themselves either. I would have to follow this punk.

He started the truck and it belched a puff of blue smoke from the tailpipe. He barely checked his mirrors before pulling away from the curb, eliciting the ire and a horn blast from a car that had to stop to avoid hitting him. It was no mystery as to why the truck's sides were caved in and scraped up. Good news for me though, as I made a left turn and fell in behind the car that nearly hit him. If he were so careless with routine driving skills, he would be an easy tail.

He turned east on El Segundo Boulevard and headed away from the beach toward Sepulveda Boulevard. When we reached the boulevard, the car between us peeled off to make a left turn, while my runner moved over to the right lane to turn south. As we were waiting to turn I checked the view on the laptop and adjusted the bullet camera so that I had a good shot of his plate. His tags were current which was a surprise. I would have thought that surf- board wax would have trumped vehicle registration as a budget line item. A red sheet of plastic served as a surrogate lens for his left tail light and some unaccounted-for-wires hung down under the tailgate.

When the light changed, the truck sputtered, coughed, and then stalled. Runner didn't miss a beat as he restarted it on the roll, and gave a second attempt at feathering the clutch. This time he was successful, and we both began heading south. I moved over one lane from him, and fell back just enough to keep up without gathering suspicion. I doubted if he would ever look back or put anything together.

With his plate number and a good shot of him, I knew that I could have backed off on the tail, gone onto the net and used my resources to track him down. But the truck could have been borrowed, and even if it weren't, I would eventually have to brace him to find out whom he was working up for. That could make things messy and add a layer of complication to the whole process. It was just easier to find out as much as I could without human intervention.

We drove south through the towns of Manhattan, Hermosa, and Redondo Beaches respectively without any fireworks. He still was clueless that I was flanking him. At the intersection of Palos Verdes Boulevard, he slowed and turned right, the truck bucking and nearly stalling again as he came out of the turn. He was heading up into the Palos Verdes Peninsula, an exclusive area of horse stables, ocean views, and multi-million dollar homes.

At the intersection of Calle Mayor, the light turned to amber and we both began to slow down. Then, without any warning, Runner must have felt emboldened and decided he could make it. Puffs of smoke shot out of his tailpipe and he went on through. By the time I reached the intersection the light had turned red and cross traffic had begun to move. I was screwed.

"Shit!"

As traffic moved on through, I sat cursing my luck; it had been too good to be true. I could see the ass end of his junk heap as it disappeared around the corner and up into the labyrinth of windy streets that always seemed to characterize pricey neighborhoods. It was a long light and with every second that passed, I knew my chances diminished of catching up with him and picking up the tail again. I would have to track him down, and either follow him again or confront him. Neither prospect filled me with joy. I had a wild hunch though, and acted on it. I had nothing left to lose at this point.

I opened the excel sheet on the laptop, turned on my GPS unit and entered an address. As the light changed, I rolled on through, the device locating its satellite signals. In a few moments, the familiar voice of Kathy the Australian came on.

"Go point two miles and veer right onto Palos Verdes Drive West."

I obliged and followed the sweeping climb to the intersection and turned. I saw that the monitor on the GPS recognized my change in direction and updated.

"In one point three miles, turn left onto Via Monte Mar."

In spite of what Naoko said, I was a good listener and followed directions from women very well. A few minutes later I arrived at the next street and turned as instructed.

"In point one mile, turn right onto Via Lazo."

The words were barely out of Kathy's electronic mouth when Via Lazo came up quickly on my right. I slowed and turned.

"Drive point one mile and end at 7130 Via Lazo."

I ignored the final instruction and pulled over to the curb as soon as I turned. I didn't need to go any further. My hunch had been right. The yellow pick-up was parked directly in front of 7130 Via Lazo. It's driver standing on the porch of the rambling ranch styled home. Standing and talking with the runner was the blackmailer, the envelope gripped comfortably in his big hand as he smiled.

"Son-of-a-bitch!"

Bill Batty was blackmailing Marion Holtzinger.

ELEVEN

"Son of a bitch...son of a bitch...son of a bitch!"

I continued my rant as I watched the two of them conduct business casually. Bill eventually reached into his back pocket, retrieved his wallet, and handed some money to Runner.

Just as he was putting it back, he looked up in my direction and paused. Even from this distance, I could see his eyes narrow and grow cold. He looked at Runner angrily and gestured in my direction accusingly. Runner looked over and simply shrugged. He was already thinking about how much pot the money could buy him.

Bill stomped off the porch and in my direction. Normally, I would pull out a sham piece of paper from my pocket and feign that I was looking at some directions and had got twisted around, but the video camera was still mounted on the dash and running. It would be hard to explain. I whipped the wheel hard to my left and floored it, executing a nearly perfect U-turn before the front tire hit the curb and bounced over it.

Through the rear-view mirror, I could see Bill running to try to catch me. Realizing it was futile, he spun around and sprinted back to his house. A white Audi A-8 was in the driveway, along with Bill's dark blue pickup truck. I hit a hard left at the end of the block and continued on to Via Monte Mar, hoping all the time that he wasn't going to give chase.

I barely slowed as I made a right turn onto Palos Verdes Drive West, cutting off a Porsche Carrera in the process, and enduring a prolonged bleat from his wimpy little German horn. I didn't waste time with the pleasantries of flipping him off and instead floored it to get the hell out of Dodge. With any luck, I could go fast enough to keep the Porsche happy and shield myself from Bill's pursuit.

No luck; the Porsche downshifted and let loose all its turbo-charged horses as it flew by me with another anemic tweet and a one finger salute. A white Audi A-8 appeared in the distance and was closing rapidly.

I whipped a hard right onto a side-street with another Spanish name a mile long, and felt the van briefly go up on two wheels. I knew my steed was no match for the turbo-charged Audi and I would just have to evade him in the maze of streets rather than try to outrun him. I turned left onto the next street and made a hard right onto another.

"Shit!" A dead-end; I hadn't seen the sign.

I spun around at the end of the cul-de-sac and was heading back out when the Audi came screaming by me in the opposite direction. I hit the end of the block and slid left to try a backtrack maneuver. In my rear view mirror, I saw the taillights of the Audi brighten and it's hood nose down.

Back out on Palos Verdes Drive, I floored it and was praying for a cop to spot me and pull me over. But it was a weekday and the road was empty, all except for Bill Batty and myself. With the Audi closing rapidly behind me, I reached up onto the dash and turned the video camera around for no reason other than I thought it might prove valuable some day.

I glanced through the rear view mirror and saw Bill fumbling with something in his lap. He held up his cell phone a few seconds later in front of his face; he was going to try to get a picture of my rear license plate. He was only twenty feet behind me. I buried my head into the headrest and hit the brakes with all the strength I had.

A second later I heard the unmistakable sound of crunching metal and shattering glass and felt the van lunge forward as the Audi slammed into my back end, lifting me briefly. My rear window fell out and landed on the hood of his car before skittering off and onto the road. In my rear view mirror I saw the driver's side of the Audi's front windshield erupt into a giant white pillow as the air bag deployed. The Audi swerved and fishtailed all over before finally coasting to a stop on the side of the road. Steam was venting from under the buckled hood, and liquid was draining out of the front.

I hit the gas again and when I had put enough distance between us, slowed down to a respectable speed and took a quick look around. I saw a car approaching in the far distance, but he wouldn't have been able to witness the crash. Witnesses or not, Bill could have gotten a picture off before we kissed. I had to ditch the van. I reached for my cell phone, activated voice dial and spoke into it.

"Clive's Used Cars."

"Dial Clive's Used Cars?"

"Yes."

"Dialing Clive's Used Cars."

It was picked up two rings later by the proprietor himself, trying to sound pious and respectable.

"Clive's Used Cars," he said. "Clive speaking."

"It's Lou Sweeney, Clive. I need to get another vehicle."

Instantly the tone changed and I thought I felt frost forming on the phone.

"What do you mean another one? Are you going to turn in the van?"

"No. The van is gone. You're not getting it back. I need another one – different model, color, etcetera – or an SUV."

"Fuck you Lou!" he hissed. "We had a deal! I'm not giving you another car."

"Yes you are Clive...or I go to the Feds. Then you'll give up *all* your cars, as well as your license, and a couple years of your life."

"Motherfucker!" he swore.

A few seconds passed as he pondered his options, of which there were none.

"When do you need it?"

"I'll pick it up this evening. What do you have?"

"Chevy Astro-Van, 2001, dark green."

"I'll take it."

"So what happened to the Ford?" he demanded to know.

"It got stolen from the lot as far as you're concerned. As soon as I hang up you need to call the police and report it stolen. You took someone out on a test drive, they pulled over, stuck a knife to your throat and made you get out. Your cell phone had gone dead so you couldn't call until you got back to the lot. You think they were on drugs."

"What!" He said incredulously. "What if they don't believe me?"

"You're a used car salesman Clive; lying comes naturally to you."

My phone beeped that a call was coming in. It was Marion.

"Gotta go. Have the Astro-Van ready this evening Clive," I said and hung up on him. I pressed the button to answer the call from Marion.

"Wha...what's going on?" she stammered. "I just got a call from Bill at my work. He was demanding to know if I had hired a private detective. He said somebody tried to kill him!"

"Not exactly," I said.

"Not exactly!" she said, under her breath. "What the hell is that supposed to mean?"

Just then, a police car came racing up the road in the opposite direction heading towards the crash scene, its siren wailing.

"I'll tell you later Marion. What did you tell Bill?"

"I...I told him I had no idea what he was talking about and that I didn't hire any detective."

"Well then you didn't lie, did you? You can sleep well tonight."

"That's a small consolation," she said.

"Look Marion," I said, steering the conversation back to the here and now. "I need to see you as soon as you get off work. I have something very important to tell you."

"I can't tonight," she began. "I have to -"

"This isn't a request Marion," I said, cutting her off. "This isn't optional. I still have the video and will use it if I have to."

She was quiet for a long time and I couldn't tell if I had lost the connection or not.

Finally, she spoke.

"You're not a detective," she said. "You're much worse."

"And much better," I said, before hanging up.

TWELVE

"Son of a bitch! God dammed bastard! Asshole! Motherfucker..."

Marion Holtzinger had nice teeth. They were straight and white, albeit a little on the small side. Her gums looked healthy, pink, and strong. She had had some bridgework done on the number four four-four five molars, but that looked to be about it as far as construction went. So far the front incisors and laterals hadn't yellowed from her smoking. This is what I noticed as she gritted and hissed through them.

We were seated on a bench in a small park in the town of Playa del Rey. It was a nice, quiet beach community just south of, and playing second fiddle to, the pricier real estate of Marina del Rey. The park was just a short jog off of the main bike path that ran along the beach.

After sending her the info on where to meet, I headed from Palos Verdes over to the town of Wilmington, a low income, blue-collar town.

Wilmington also had a large industrial base that included oil refineries, auto salvage yards, and metals recycling facilities, one of which was Garcia Reclamation.

I had stepped in to help the Garcia family a few years back, when a Croatian mob from nearby San Pedro had decided they would like a cut of their thriving business. It just so happened that the chief mobster had a son that was a closeted gay. I threatened to drag him out of it, pink tights and all, if they didn't back down. The mob quickly changed gears and decided to focus on selling stolen cargo containers instead.

Hector Garcia, the oldest son, helped me personally, and within ten minutes the Mini-van was reduced to a washing machine sized hunk of steel, and plastic, and just may have ended up as a part of the E-reader your using right now.

I had just enough time after leaving Wilmington to take a taxi home, change clothes, and grab my bike, to ride up and meet with Marion. I synched the video of the runner, my tail, and the money shot of Bill, to my phone, omitting the footage of the crash scene. I played it for her as soon as we sat down, and that's when her tirade began.

She stopped swearing just long enough to fumble in her purse for her cigarettes. She found the pack, and extracted one with trembling hands. I grabbed her lighter and lit it for her. She took in a huge drag, held it for a bit, and then blew it upward. The word "ass-hole" came out with the exhale of gray smoke. A jogger ran by at the same moment and turned to look at her as she said it.

"Are you going to tell me what this is all about Marion?"

She took another inhale, slowly. She looked over her cigarette at me. I didn't think she was reconsidering. She looked like someone who had thrown in the towel. Like she was beaten, had nothing left to lose.

"What the hell," she said, exhaling out of the corner of her mouth.

I waited.

She looked away toward the small pond in the middle of the park. An older man was playing with a young boy, of about three years old, that I assumed was his grandson. They had a bag of bread and were tearing off hunks to throw to a noisy group of ducks that had come for the handout. The little boy squealed with delight and ran for grandpa's protection anytime one of the ducks got too close. A second later, he would be throwing himself right back into harm's way. Marion didn't even see them.

"I went to work about two years ago for a small company that did energy trading," she began.

"That was Zeus Investments Limited, correct?"

She stopped suddenly and looked at me. "How did you...?"

She turned away and took another pull on the cigarette.

"That's right," she snorted, smoke flowing from her lips. "You know everything about me."

"Not everything. That's why we're here. Tell me about Zeus."

She nodded, "Okay. But I guess I should give you a little background first. Why I went to work there, how I got stuck there, etcetera."

She took another drag, stared off toward the pond, exhaled, then leaned forward and put her cigarette out on the ground with the toe of her pumps. She was wearing a red V- neck sweater and beige slacks. Everything fit snugly and wrapped her lithe body nicely.

"Anyway...like I said; I went to work with them about two years ago. I have a CPA License, I've kept it current, but I hadn't used it for years. My husband and I have a son. He was born with mild epilepsy and required a lot of attention. I became a stay-at-home mom and took care of him. He did pretty well, considering. We had him in special classes, programs – the works. It was a lot of effort, but I'm proud to say that he became a functional, reasonably independent member of society."

She glanced over at me. I felt that approval of her performance was apropos for the moment. I nodded.

"Sounds like you did a great job."

She nodded humbly and turned back to the pond. The man and young boy were out of bread, and walking away from the edge of the water. The ducks, sensing a loss of their entitlement, were following them and protesting bitterly.

"And so, after eighteen years of care-taking, I was ready to get out of the house and pick up again with my career. We didn't need the money, I was just ready to get out and join the real world. I saw the Zeus ad for a receptionist-slash-bookkeeper online, and sent in my resume. I figured that I didn't want to dive back in too deep to begin with, and that it would be a good to start slow. Also, it was in Long Beach, and our son was going to school at Cal State at the time. It seemed perfect."

She reached into her purse and pulled out her cigarettes again. She sat staring at the pack in her hand for a long time, considering the temptation. Finally, she dropped it back into her purse and set the bag down on the bench, where it would take more effort to retrieve.

"I liked Zeus at first," she continued. "It was a small office. Just myself and Rick Harris, the owner. He did energy trading in all sorts of things, gasoline futures being one of them. I had never heard of that before I went to work for him. Like most people, I always thought that only oil was traded, not the finished product."

I nodded patiently. I didn't tell her that a lot of this was old news to me. I had gone through her employment records, as well as her son's medical records.

"That was where I first met Bill. He was a creep - then and obviously now. He wasn't on the payroll, but came in quite a bit to talk to Rick, always leering at me or trying to make time. They would have lots of closed-door private conversations, and I knew that Bill had some sort of connection to the oil industry."

"He had worked in it," I said. "And then became some sort of a big wheel in the refinery workers union. Right?"

She nodded, getting used to the fact that I already had mined quite a bit of info.

"The Oil Workers International Union," she said. "I didn't know what he did there at the time or how it connected to Zeus. By the time I figured it out, it was too late."

Getting to the meat, I thought.

"So I pretty much ignored him and concentrated on my job. There was a lot to learn and Rick was really helpful. He schooled me on the basics of commodity investing: trading on margins, puts, calls, and everything else to do with it. How, if you thought gasoline prices were going to rise, you could buy a 'call' option. It all became fascinating and exciting. I was seeing the cash flow going through the office and knew that there was money to be made. Rick seemed to have the Midas Touch."

Giving in to temptation, she finally reached for her purse and shook a cigarette out of the pack. She lit it with hands that I noticed weren't shaking anymore, and then took a few slow pulls. She held it lightly in her hand and it stuck out like the bowsprit of a sailboat.

"About a year ago my mom died and I inherited some money. It wasn't a whole lot; she didn't have much. And because we were doing well with my husband's income and mine, I decided to invest it into the gasoline futures market. My husband was fine with it, and said that it was my "play money" and I could do whatever I wanted with it. I talked to Rick and he helped me set up a trading account and get started. He said he felt very good about the market. "Bullish" was the term he used."

"I only invested a little of it at first, and, following Rick's advice, did well on my trades. I guess I was feeling pretty cocky and decided to go all-in on my next trade."

She turned to stare right at me, "That was my big mistake."

I nodded and waited.

"My husband got sick – real sick. And he had to quit working.

A young couple walked by us, holding hands. The man was talking loudly and in a condescending tone. I thought he was chastising the woman for something until I realized that he has was talking to someone else on his hands-free; what a world.

"Pretty soon we were down to just my income. His sick-time had run out and the short-term disability hardly paid anything. We also had mounting medical bills. I tried to pull my money back out of the trade I had made, but I couldn't do it without incurring a huge penalty. Rick kept saying, "Just wait. Just wait," like he knew something."

"Insider trading?" I asked.

"Similar, but not exactly. I don't know if you know much about the refining side of the oil industry, but the supply is tight – super tight. In 1988, there were thirty-four refineries operating in California, now there are only fourteen. And the demand has grown. What this means is that any time any one of the fourteen have an upset that causes them to shut down unexpectedly, it affects the entire gasoline market in a negative way."

"Supply and demand," I said.

"Exactly. One refinery "falling down," as they

say, can easily spike the price of gasoline by ten cents a gallon on the spot market, depending on the time of year. That doesn't sound like much, but we're talking here about trading on margin. And a small investment can yield hundreds of thousands of dollars in profits if you guess correctly."

I nodded. I was beginning to understand the Zeus "Midas Touch."

"Was Bill feeding Rick information about the refineries?"

She took a final drag on her cigarette and put it out. She nodded.

"Since he had some connection to the union and the workers, he could feed Rick all kinds of information about unexpected shutdowns to facilities, but one in particular."

"Which one?"

"The Champion Refinery in Torrance."

I knew the place; it was enormous. "So Bill had someone on the inside of Champion supplying him with information?"

"Yes. But that's not all that unusual. I soon learned that some of the more unscrupulous traders try to get info about the duration and the magnitude of any issues going on inside of these places. 'Knowledge is power', and all that sort of stuff. They'd pump the workers, and the contractors and suppliers, for any information they could get and try to piece it together. It helped them calculate the price ceilings and how long they'd stay elevated. I'm not even sure if it's illegal..."

She turned to stare at me, "...But what Rick and Bill were doing certainly was."

Her cell phone went off in her purse. She pulled it out and took a look at the display.

"I'm sorry," she said. "I have to get this. It's my son."

I stood up and walked away to give her a little privacy. As it was, I could still hear parts of the one sided conversation, as well as the tone. Her son was obviously upset about something and Marion tried to reassure him.

"...I know honey," she said. "I know...just do what you can...I know...I'll be home...Yes...I'll...I'll be home as soon as I can."

She turned the phone off and dropped it back into her purse. I returned to the bench. In just a couple of minutes, she looked to have aged five years. She sat staring off into the middle distance, shoulders slumping, her face slack. A spirit drained. She wouldn't look at me.

"I have to leave soon," she said flatly.

I nodded, then prompted her to finish. "Rick and Bill, Marion," I said. "What were they doing that was illegal?"

"Sabotage," she said.

"Sabotage? Of the facilities?"

She nodded slowly. "Champion. They had someone on the inside. They'd closed a valve or opened one, or turned something on or off when it wasn't supposed to. I don't know how they did it, but they could bring the place to its knees. That was why Rick kept telling me to 'stay in the game' when I wanted to exit my trade. Rather than just get the inside dope on what was going on after an upset, Zeus decided to kick it up to a notch by buying the option and then causing the problem."

"Do you have any proof Marion? This is quite an accusation."

She nodded slowly, as if it was painful for her to move.

"During the time of my last trade, the office was quite abuzz. Rick was getting lots of calls on his cell, I think from Bill, and was closing his doors a lot. Bill was popping in all the time and meeting with him. They were both acting very cagey and anxious, like they couldn't wait for the other shoe to drop. I started to get nervous about the whole thing."

She took a deep breath, her small chest rising.

"One day I was leaving for lunch just as Bill was coming through the door. He turned sideways to let me through, but made sure our bodies kind of rubbed up against each other. It was gross. I couldn't wait to get out of there. Then I realized I had forgotten my cell phone in my desk. I went back in to get it and Rick's door was open. They didn't know I had come back, and I could hear them talking. Bill was telling Rick, 'It's all set for Tuesday night.'"

"Rick responded with, 'You're sure he knows what he's doing?'"

"Bill laughed and said, 'No problem. He's a loser, but he knows what to do. That place is going to drop like a rock.'"

She turned toward me with a look of shame on her face "That Tuesday night the Champion facility went down and stayed down for eight days. It cost the facility millions of dollars in repairs and lost profits, and the price of gasoline on the spot market went up eight and half cents a gallon. We all made money – including me. Worst of all, it caused a fire and two of the workers got injured. I felt so ashamed and dirty about the whole thing."

She took another deep breath and held it. Her face tightened. She swallowed. From the edges of her sunglasses, I could see the corners of her eyes squint as she fought back tears.

"It's not your fault Marion," I said. "You weren't aware of any of this at the time."

Her head slumped. "I know," she choked out. "I tried to get out afterward, and that's when the whole thing started with Bill."

"Tell me about it," I said, trying to keep the flow going before she fell completely to pieces.

Her head rose back up and she exhaled heavily, like it took a Herculean effort to do so. She was going to get through this, she decided.

"I knew I had to get out, before someone got wise to the shenanigans, and I could be investigated. I started to look for other jobs – legitimate jobs. I saw one for a CPA at a major company, Sunshine Foods, the one I work at now. It had good pay, benefits - the whole thing. I put in for it and knew I had a good chance of getting it."

"What happened next?"

"Bill and Rick had a falling out. Bill knew that Rick made a ton of money on the trade when they sabotaged the facility. He probably paid Bill a flat rate for getting it orchestrated. Now Bill wanted more and was willing to rat out Rick if he didn't get more."

"Simple blackmail," I stated. "Did Rick cave in to Bill's demands?"

She nodded.

"In the end, Rick threw some more money at Bill, and that seemed to satisfy him."

"How did you find out about all of this Marion?"

"Bill told me. He said that since he, Bill, wasn't on the payroll and hadn't invested in the trade, that he couldn't be connected to the whole thing, but Rick could."

She turned her head slowly toward me, "And so could I."

* * *

We sat staring at each other for what seemed like a long time. The park had gotten very quiet, very distant. It was like we weren't even in it physically, but were just ghosts passing through, spending a little time with the mere mortals while they moved about oblivious to our existence. I had already pieced the rest of the story together.

"And then Bill told you that if you went to bed with him, he would leave you out of it. Right Marion?"

The dam broke. Her face scrunched up and she began to shudder. Tears streamed down the sides of her face, turning slightly beige from her make-up. She fell toward me and I caught her in my arms. Her whole body convulsed uncontrollably as I held her tight against my chest.

"I didn't want to!" she sobbed. "I really didn't want to! He's just so...repulsive! But I was right in the middle of my background check with Sunshine Foods, and if this would have come out, innocent or not, it would have derailed the whole thing, and they would have dropped me like a hot potato. We needed the money. My husband still couldn't go back to work, and my son had already quit school to take care of him while I worked. Our bills were racking up and we were at risk of losing our house!"

She pulled away from my grasp and sat up, her face streaked with tinted tears, her voice hot.

"I had to do it!" she bellowed. "I had to!"

"I know Marion," I said. "Like I told you, I could read it from the expression on your face on the video."

I pulled a bandana from the rear pocket of my cycling jersey and wiped her face as best I could. She took it out of my hands and continued the job. I stood up and stepped away, absorbing, thinking.

From behind me I heard her hiss in a steely voice, "I would kill him if I could," she said. "You know I would. I would do anything to end this nightmare!"

I turned back towards her.

"I told you Marion, killing him would just bring more heat down on you. I know it would feel good, but it would be short-lived."

She sighed and began to cry again. "So it's hopeless then. I'm just totally fucked forever."

"I didn't say that. I just said that we weren't going to kill him."

She clutched the bandana tightly in her hands and looked up at me with the slightest glimmer of hope on her face.

"We?" she said.

I nodded at her and she smiled.

"We're going to do something much better," I said.

THIRTEEN

Marion and I stayed in the park for another half-hour or so. Her son had called again, agitated and disturbed, and Naoko had left me a voice mail as well as a text, wondering where the heck I was, and what we were going to do tonight. Marion caught me up with as much detail as she could in the remaining time, but I would need a lot more from her. I told her I needed to know everything I could about Zeus, Rick Harris, Bill Batty, and the inside person at the Champion Refinery, a man she had never met, but had overheard Bill and Rick refer to as "Walker" – most likely a last, as opposed to a first, name. I would also need a crash course in the art/science/voodoo of energy trading. She, in turn, pressed me for details about what I was going to do. I told her that I would tell her in due time. Due time as in, whenever I figured out what the heck I was going to do. I gave her a different cell number to call, as well as a new e-mail, to stay in touch with me.

We parted awkwardly, not knowing whether to shake hands, hug, or simply walk away. We were partners now, as opposed to adversaries. In the end, I grabbed my bike and rolled it between us, setting the tone and wondering why I had done it. Strapping on my helmet I told her to send me whatever new information she could think of, no matter how insignificant she thought it may be.

"I'll be in touch," I called out as I pedaled away. She didn't hear me, as she was already on her cell phone, calling home I guessed. I called Naoko and talked to her as I rode home.

Lately, I had been getting pressed to take her out for a nice dinner on the town. While I thought tonight might be an opportune time - due to the fact I had nothing planned or defrosted - in the end I begged off from seeing her at all tonight. This of course, elicited more of her wrath for a second day in a row. But it had been a long, crazy day and my head was swimming with facts and fiction, scenarios and angles, villains and victims. I still had a lot to learn, and I had a lot of work ahead of me. I needed to be alone.

The sun was close to setting over the Pacific by the time I rode up to the condo. I took a quick shower, grabbed a beer out of the fridge, and stepped out onto my balcony to watch the finale of yet another day. Just enough late afternoon clouds had drifted in to set the stage for a nice show. This fact wasn't lost on others as the walking path four stories below me began to fill up with people milling about, waiting to drink in the spectacle.

Before long, the sky tinged a bright orange over the western horizon, the sun slipping lower into the water, its disc beginning to elongate and flatten. The clouds slowly deepened to a dull orange color, and then finally morphed to a blood red. A silver-skinned jet, high in the western sky above us, was illuminated brightly as we slipped into darkness five miles below. It was free and we were bound.

The show lasted only a few minutes but was endless in its infinity. Move a few miles west and you would see it occur all over again. Move halfway around the world and you would witness it's inverse as a new day began. The sun never really rose or set, like everything else in our insignificant lives; it was only our perspective.

The gawkers and the lovers, and the people that interrupted their bike-rides or runs just long enough to see the show, picked up and moved on slowly. I grabbed another beer, switched on the balcony light and sat down in a chair with a mechanical pencil and a long legal pad. It was a nice night and I might as well enjoy it while I was working.

I turned the pad sideways and started recording what I already knew about the situation, or what I accepted as fact from Marion. I drew a box in the middle and towards the top of the page with the word "Zeus" written in it. Under the word Zeus, and in the same box, I wrote the name Rick Harris. Under Rick's name I wrote the word "others" with a question mark next to it.

Below this, and to the left, I drew another box with the words "Champion Oil" in it. Under this went the name "Walker," preceded by a blank line to fill in Walker's first name when I discovered it. Another question mark went into the blank in the mean time. I added the word "others" next to this as well.

A third box was drawn with the name Bill Batty in it. I drew it below and to the right of, the Zeus box. I drew arrows going both ways from the Zeus box and the Batty box, and then did the same with the Batty box to the Champion Oil box, illustrating what I assumed to be the lines of communication and information flow.

I stared at it for a second realizing that it wasn't truly representative, then erased the "Walker" name and the word "other" from under the word Champion and put them into their own boxes under Champion's. I erased and then redrew the arrows until they shot accurately back and forth from Zeus to Bill, and then from Bill to Walker and company. I made an assumption that Rick Harris never paid the inside guy at Champion directly, and added dollar signs on the arrows flowing from Zeus to Bill, and then passing through from Bill to Walker et al.

Again, I realized that something might not be completely accurate and erased the dollar sign flowing from Bill to Walker, and replaced it with a question mark. The person or persons inside Champion might be sabotaging the equipment for financial gains, but then again, they could be doing it for revenge or some other Ludditian cause-celeb. Finally, I studied the diagram one more time and satisfied, put a big circle around the whole affair and wrote the words "Gasoline Futures Market" within the circle. I sat looking at it for a long moment and realized I didn't have much. It was a basic conspiracy between several parties, but didn't come close to illustrating the malfeasance and machinations that were the backbone of their enterprise. I really knew nothing or no one. I put a big bold question mark inside the circle, drained my beer, and stepped inside the condo. I went to my laptop and logged onto the Emperium web site. It was time to go information mining and start filling in the blanks.

I decided to start with Bill Batty as he was the person I knew the most about at this point, And then I would work my way down through Rick Harris and Mr. Walker. I flipped to the next page of the legal pad and set it on the desk next to me. I knew that I would have more questions the deeper I went, and wanted to capture them for further follow up.

In the last half hour we had talked in the park, Marion had already addressed one of the more vexing mysteries for me. Namely, how could a guy like Bill, with marginal employment status, afford to live in Palos Verdes, a prime real estate area with horse trails, ocean views, and home prices that routinely started at the million-dollar mark? The answer was a simple and a classic one; he had married money. I opened the Excel file I had on Bill and checked out his wife's name. Through some cross-referencing of Social Security Numbers on the Emperium site, I found out that Allison Mary Batty had originally been Allison Mary Sullivan. She was one of four Sullivan siblings, and an heir apparent to the Sullivan TV and Appliance Kingdom.

It was an easy enough scenario to visualize, as it happened all too often in the land of milk and honey. Old Man Sullivan launches his empire umpteen years ago with a dollar and a dream. He works endless hours through the years, slaving away to build and grow his business. His kids in the meantime lead privileged lives, and far into adulthood are still feeding at the teat. Some will stay clinging forever, and others, naively thinking they are weaned, will want management of the whole cow, killing it and a lifetime of toil in the process.

I Googled Allison Mary Batty and Allison Mary Sullivan to find any recent pictures of her and found several examples. Many of these were from the society pages of the local newspapers where she was mugging for the camera while attending charity and other black-tie social events. Several of the pictures included Bill as he stood next to her self-consciously, grimacing like his underpants were too tight.

Allison Mary Batty nee Sullivan was an unattractive and plain woman with eyes too far apart, a nose that was too small, and hips that were too big. She would have trouble attracting even the most myopic of men and would have died a lonely, albeit comfortable life, as the spinster daughter of a self-made millionaire, had it not been for the wiles of a leach like Bill Batty.

While I was at it, I looked for prior marriages for both Bill and Allison. Bill had two: The first, lasting 12 years and producing a son now twenty-three years old, and serving his country in the US Army; The second, bearing no offspring, and lasting only three years before ending in divorce. Not surprisingly, Allison had no prior marriages or name changes that I could find, and had married Bill approximately three years ago at the ripe age of 46. They had no children.

I wrote the names of Bill's previous wives onto the sheet with the word follow-up? next to them, and then cut and pasted all the rest of the info into the Excel sheet in the column under Bill's marital status, and moved on. For now, Allison Mary Batty would not be considered a co-conspirator in project Zeus.

I returned the focus of my efforts to Bill and soon had a dossier' that painted an ignominious and checkered past. Besides a couple of failed marriages, he also had a spotty work record and a couple of minor scrapes with the law. He started work with the Champion Oil Company in1992 and voluntarily resigned eleven years later. This was suspicious, as jobs in the oil industry were highly coveted for their good pay and benefits without generally requiring a college degree – which Bill was lacking. This meant that his departure from Champion could have been the result of a performance or disciplinary issue that resulted in an option to either voluntarily resign, or be terminated, a common practice at many larger companies wishing to avoid litigation. Having at least the good sense to recognize when he was painted in a corner, he could have wisely chosen this option. I made another note on the legal pad to follow up on his "resignation" from Champion.

After his stint at Champion, he had a string of short-term jobs with various companies that contracted for oil field services before becoming a full-time employee of the Oil Workers of America Union. His job title was, "Membership Organizer," and he was employed with the union up until he voluntarily resigned from this position about three years ago, not long after he had married Allison Mary. Why run a dairy farm when you were getting milk for free?

His scrapes with the law had been relatively minor, but were still noteworthy. In his illustrious life, he had had two drunk driving convictions, the most recent seven years ago, his first, about thirteen years prior to that. He also had a restraining order filed against him by his second wife, which had since expired. And fourteen years ago, he had an assault charge leveled against him, which was later dropped. Old Billy Boy was a busy guy when it came to the courts, divorce or otherwise.

The clock on my laptop read 10:11 p.m. Without realizing it, I had already been at this for several hours. Besides being weary and tired from the day, I was hungry as well. There were four pieces of leftover pizza in the refrigerator and I popped two of them into the microwave. I ate them standing over the kitchen counter and drank a glass of milk to wash them down.

As I was putting everything into the dishwasher, my personal cell phone went off, it was Naoko.

"Hi," I said.

"Hi," she said in a strangely quiet voice. "Are you busy?"

"Just taking a little break. What are you up to?"

"Thinking."

"About what?"

"Us."

I probably paused a nanosecond too long.

"What about us?" I prompted.

"Is there someone else Jack?"

FOURTEEN

I didn't fall over, drop the phone, or vomit. Instead I stood motionless in the kitchen, my feet glued to the floor. For some reason I couldn't fathom, my mind flashed unintentionally to Marion. Before I could dwell on her too long, I forced the image from my head, shaking it in the process.

"No!" I protested maybe a little bit too strongly. "Why do you say that?"

"I don't know. You just seem kind of ...distant lately."

"Distant?"

"Yes. The other night when I came over, you seemed like you weren't really listening to me when we were talking and going through our days."

"Yes I was Naoko," I said. Yet for the life of me, I couldn't remember what she had told me.

"And even when we made love, you seemed distracted"

"Distracted?"

I heard my own voice in the phone and realized how phony I sounded. I was repeating every statement and observation she made with a question. It was a rank amateur's way to try to cover up a lie by constantly parroting everything that was said. I'd heard it a million times. I just never thought I would be the one on the delivery side.

"Listen Naoko, there's nobody else. You're the only one. But I'm very busy right now. I told you that. I've had some really long days and I still have work to do tonight."

"I know," she purred, "But I just miss you."

"And I miss you, I just have to work on this case right now."

"Well, what is it? Can't you at least tell me what it's about?"

"You know the rules sweety."

She huffed and the sound of her voice flattened considerably.

"Yes," she said. "I guess I do."

I knew the tone. I had to move from a defensive posture to a damage control mode.

"Listen, how about meeting for lunch tomorrow? We can see each other then and talk."

There was a long pause, I thought I had lost the connection.

"Naoko? Naoko?"

"Okay," she finally said. "I have a cystectomy at ten. So I should be done and cleaned up by twelve-thirty. I could meet you around one."

"Great," I said, putting as much enthusiasm into my voice as possible without sounding patronizing. "I'll see you then."

"Good night Jack. I'll see you tomorrow."

She hung up. No kissing sounds, no "Muuuuaaahhhs." It was all business. She was the appointment desk and I'd just been confirmed for my proctologist exam. I stood with the phone to my ear, listening to its hollow emptiness. The refrigerator was humming in the kitchen, and a couple somewhere out on the beach were having sex and braving a sand-rash.

"What the hell?" I said to myself.

I snapped the phone shut and returned to the laptop. The data on Bill Batty was still up on the screen. I re-read it, and then saved the file.

I looked at the clock again...it was just past eleven. What did modern man do? He looked at a clock to tell him if it was time to eat, or to go to bed. Weren't our bodies completely capable of letting us know if we were hungry or tired? I was exhausted; there was no doubt about it. But I knew if I went to bed now it would just be a waste of time. My head would churn with thoughts about Naoko and what she had said. When in doubt One Eyed Jack, just keep working. At least you'll have something to show for your lack of sleep.

I launched the spy-ware application and copied and pasted the IP address of the Batty's modem into the search field. If his computer was up and running, I could look inside and snoop around at will. Even if it wasn't on, I could force a boot and the Battys would think that they had either forgotten to turn it off, or that they had a tech-savvy poltergeist in occupancy.

The Battys had three computers connected to the modem. One of them was on and someone was on the Internet. Based upon the last digits of the IP address, it was Bill's computer. I clicked on the magnifying glass icon in the program's taskbar to "observe activity" and a real-time screen image of unit's desktop came up.

It was Bill all right. He was online and engaged in a flirty chat session with a woman named Teresa. I moved off of his desktop and navigated to his e-mail accounts. He had three: two Yahoo accounts, and one Hotmail. I opened up the contact list of the first Yahoo account and began looking for anything with the name "Walker" in it.

The first Yahoo account had no Walker as even the first or second name listed, and no addresses with even a mysterious "W" in the contact info. Instead, there were a couple of "Batty" names as well as several "Sullivans" and a few other random names that meant nothing to me. It appeared to be a personal e-mail list of friends and family. I downloaded it and saved it into a Word document titled Bill's E-mails.

The second Yahoo account had a slightly more nefarious look to it. It contained only two entries in the contact list. One was for Rick Harris at the Zeus Investments web site, the other was apparently Rick's personal e-mail. Why Billy Boy thought he would gain some level of security by having an account with just two names in it was a mystery to me. I cut and pasted the information into the Word doc. and went into his In-Box. The folder contained no items, so I clicked on the Sent. It was empty.

The same was true with the Draft, Spam and, Trash folders. At least he took out the garbage when he should.

He had no other miscellaneous folders in this account and so I moved onto the Hotmail account.

The Hotmail contact list was a bonanza – at least if you were looking for female connections on the Internet. All of the contacts' first names were female, and some had cell and office phone numbers attached to them. Marion's was in there as well. Again, I saw no entries that could even remotely be construed as, or a derivative of, the name Walker. I didn't bother to copy and paste the names and moved on.

His personal document folders contained only four sub-folders. The first was labeled House Stuff and contained e-mails from contractors doing work on the Batty Homestead. There was also an angry letter to a company from which he had apparently bought a tank-less water heater and been less than satisfied. A few downloaded PDFs with product instructions, and warranty information rounded out the file.

I closed the folder and moved onto the next, which was labeled Investments. To my surprise it was empty. I sat for a while staring at the white screen, a space occupied only by my obedient cursor. The couple on the beach was apparently post-coital and all I heard was an occasional crash of the waves. I moved the cursor around in random circles and figure eight's because that's what you did with your cursor on a screen devoid of icons. What had been in here?

I clicked on the back arrow into the main

folder and went to the label titled Private. Certainly this would yield some treasures. The folder contained numerous Word docs. with strange titles. Some of the names were 'Tuxedo Nights', 'Velvet Moon', and 'Reflections from the Sky'. I opened one at random. It was poetry, Bill Batty's poetry. Who would have thought? For some crazy reason, I read it and found it wasn't too bad. I had never composed a piece of poetry in my life and never would. I gave my adversary a little credit...very little. It wouldn't last.

I closed the folder and moved on to the final one, the one labeled Union Business. It was anything but, and was filled with porn, stills and video. Filth in every format under the digital sun. I opened one and saw a girl of questionable age engaged in an act that most adult women would not submit to. I closed it quickly and scanned some of the other file names. Big as life, about halfway down the page was an MP-4 labeled "Marion." I sat staring at the icon and its simple title for a long time.

"I'm gonna get you, you son of a bitch!"

I briefly entertained the thought about wiping out his whole treasure-trove: his porn, his contact lists - maybe even wipe his entire hard drive, but then I thought better of it. Vengeance is always better when it waits. Instead I navigated back to his desktop screen and observed as he continued his animated discussion with his new friend on IM.

Teresa: "so how long have u been an airline pilot?"

Bill: " 15 yrs."

Teresa: "it must b an exciting life!"

Bill: "it is. im flying 2 Paris next week."

Teresa: "Paris! Wow! im envious!"

Bill: "and Rio the following week. it gets lonely though. maybe we could get 2gether when im between flights."

Teresa: "that would be gr8! u can tell me all about your globetrotting life. LOL"

Airline pilot! Jesus Christ!

If Pinocchio would have had internet access, his proboscis would have been as long as the Alaskan Pipeline! It was all I could do to not throw-up. I was really beginning to despise this clown. I moved my cursor over to the "Close" icon in the upper right corner of the messenger application box and left it hovering.

Teresa: "i check my vm several times a day so if you don't get me, leave a msg. and i'll get back to you as soon as i can. my number is..."

Sorry lover boy.

I clicked the box and the window closed. Teresa, whomever she was, had disappeared into the ether world and Billy Boy had no number to show for all of his beguiling efforts. In a second or so, I could see his cursor frantically whipping around the screen and trying to re-establish a connection. I closed it down every time it would start to launch.

I went to the Start Menu and navigated my way to the Control Panel and the Add or Remove Hardware. I uninstalled his modem driver. No more WWW for Billy Boy until he got tired of trying and performed a reboot.

I disconnected from the modem and rubbed my eyes. I could start on Rick Harris tonight or I could not. I could also dive off my balcony and swim across the Pacific or I could not. Instead, I went to bed, my mind whirling like a blender with people and their motivations: Bill, Naoko, Rick Harris, Marion and the mysterious Mr. Walker. I tossed and turned for several hours before drifting off into a fitful sleep. When I finally did, I dreamt of Pinocchio at the controls of a 747. I was on board. Worst of all; I was in coach.

FIFTEEN

"Champion Oil Refinery. How may I direct your call?"

The voice was female, probably young, and obviously bored.

"Mr. Walker please."

"Steven Walker, Charles Walker, or Nathaniel Walker?"

"I'm not sure Ma'am. My assistant forgot to write down the first name. She just said it was very important I call -."

"You probably want Nathaniel Walker," she said sharply. "Stand by while I connect you."

As she was pushing buttons, I wrote down the given names of all three Walkers just in case I wasn't going to be connected to the correct one. I had a starting point at least.

The line went silent for a moment, then to some 80's music I knew but didn't know, then it begin to ring on the other end. The line picked up in two rings.

"Main Crude Unit!" a man's voice bellowed. He had to speak loud as there was a riot of sound in the background. I could hear the crackle of radio transmissions, alarms beeping urgently, as well as the general boisterousness that comes with blue-collared men working together in a confined area. I could tell it was a Control House for one of the facility's units.

"Nathaniel Walker please."

"Hold on."

He must have pulled the handset away from his mouth and cupped it with his hand, although not enough. I could hear a muted conversation mixed in with the din.

"Who is it?" another man asked the man I was speaking to.

"Another guy for Nate."

"Tell him he's in the field doing his readings and that he'll have to call back."

The receiver was uncovered just as a roar of laughter went up in the background. It sounded like a frat party on steroids.

"He's out in the field now. You'll have to call back."

"Okay," I said and the man hung up, but not before I heard another man in the distant background yell out, laughing, "Because it's your fucking job asshole!"

I hung up and took another sip of coffee. It was my second of the day. I had woken at about eight this morning. Bright shafts of sunlight were pushing through the windows and telling me the sun had behaved and come up on the other side of the world. My eyes felt like they had been scrubbed with steel wool and I needed a ride, a shower, some breakfast, and a new life. But I needed answers first.

I had recorded the entire phone call, from the receptionist through to the Control House personnel. A voice stress analyzer program was running on my computer and my phone was synced to it. The program had analyzed every pause, inflection, change of pitch, and minor tremor in the speech patterns of the people I had spoken to. It was the equivalent of the poor-man's polygraph machine. Levels of deception or outright lies could be detected by it.

As I would have expected, there were no traces of stress in the receptionist's voice. In fact, the graph showed mostly flat throughout our brief exchange. But the two conversations from the Control House personnel showed signs of slight deception.

So, Nate Walker works in the Control House of the refinery's main crude unit and receives lots of calls. So many calls in fact, that the company operator doesn't waste time routing any generic queries for a "Mr. Walker" to anyone but him. And his co-workers appear to be stretching the truth a bit to cover for him. Interesting. I'd try again in a couple of hours.

I dialed the main number of the Champion Refinery again. After the recorded instructions to dial the extension of the person I was trying to reach ran their course, I waited on the line and got the same bored receptionist. She recited her greeting once again with all the cheer of an autopsy report being read, and I asked for the extensions for both Steven and Charles Walker. She gave them to me and then asked if she could connect me with either one of them. Without going through the rather scientific process of a game of eenie-meenie-miny-mo, I asked to be connected to Steven Walker, just because Steven had been my father's name.

It must have been the morning for Stevens, because I heard Steven Tyler of Aerosmith belt out a line from "Walk this Way" before the phone began to ring. It rang so many times that I thought it would go to voice mail. Finally a man picked it up, he was breathless and sounded as if he had lunged at the phone.

"Human Resources - Steve Walker."

"Hi Steve. It's Bill."

There was a pause and a moment of confusion.

"Bill? Bill who?"

The real time graph from the stress analyzer showed no change.

"Bill Batty."

There was a momentary pause, not of a stalling nature, but of a searching nature, the type that occurred when you were trying to avoid embarrassment because you were supposed to remember someone's name, but couldn't.

"I'm sorry Mr. Batty. I'm afraid I can't place the name."

Flat line, no lying going on here.

"Ok," I said. "Maybe I have the wrong Mr. Walker. Is there a Nathaniel Walker at the facility?"

"Yeeesssss," Steven Walker said very slowly. There was caution in his voice, and trepidation. The graph moved up.

"Maybe he's the one I need to talk to," I said.

"Yes. Maybe so."

I thanked him for his time and hung up.

I dialed the number for Charles Walker and waited through about six rings. A recording finally came on informing me that Charles Walker would be out of the office for the week, and that I should direct any questions regarding order expediting to Samantha Riley. So much for Charles Walker.

I zapped an instant breakfast sandwich in the microwave, and sat down with it and a refill of my coffee, in front of my laptop. Nathaniel Walker seemed to be the best candidate for any shenanigans at Champion Oil, and I decided to concentrate my efforts on him for the time being. It would be too soon to call the Control House back, so after making some notes on my laptop and saving the voice stress graphs, I decided to change gears.

Through the Emperium database, I queried the name Rick Harris and came up with several hits. I filtered them down based upon age and location until I came up with the one that appeared to be the most promising. I hit the tax returns first and saw that for the past two years this Rick Harris had listed his occupation as Energy Trader.

Bingo.

I finished my breakfast, and over the next hour or so, dug into the life of Mr. Richard Mathew Harris. He was 32, grew up in Huntington Beach, California, and had an MBA from Cal State Fullerton. He drove an eight-series BMW (leased), lived in rented condo in Belmont Shores, and was unmarried. I checked his profile on LinkedIn and saw his profile picture. He was handsome in a "boy next door" way and had dark wavy hair, green eyes and a nice smile. In all, he fit the stereotype of the successful yuppie to a tee. But, like most conspicuous consumers, it was more illusion than reality.

Rick's father, Daniel Harris, had invented a special filter for diesel fueled trucks back in 1971. The device had been awarded a patent and was instantly a success. He had built a successful company around it, and several other devices, targeting the diesel trucking industry. There was a website, Harrisfilters.com, and I browsed around it. Besides old man Harris, two other people named Harris worked at the company. One was listed as Vice President in charge of production, and the other was the company's CFO. I cross-referenced the names through Emperium and found that they were both Rick's older brothers.

I returned to Rick Harris's tax returns and went back several years. Rick had worked at Harris Filters since the time he was sixteen years old, but had left the company and started out on his own in his early twenties. He was listed as CEO and sole proprietor of a dot-com company that had gone bust with all the rest in 2001. This was followed by several failed multi-level marketing schemes, and then finally, he rode the real estate bubble/mortgaged back securities catastrophe into oblivion in 2008. His income throughout the years reflected his roller-coaster ride of successes and failures, and it was only on his last tax return, as an Energy Trader, that he finally hit the magic six-figure mark. I wondered how much of it was due to the Champion Oil scheme.

I leaned back in the chair and took a sip of coffee. It had gone cold and I set the cup back down without bothering to refill it or warm it in the microwave. I had enough caffeine for the day and was starting to feel some jitters.

I glanced at the clock. It was just about ten. If Nate Walker had been out in the plant doing his work, he might be back in the Control House by now. A cold call might yield the same evasive results and so I decided to try a new tactic.

Marion had given me Bill's cell phone number and I loaded a spoof number into my cell phone before calling it. Bill answered in two rings and I switched on the voice stress analyzer.

"Hello."

The voice was breathy, harsh, and impatient. I watched it track on the graph on my screen.

"Hi Mr. Batty. This is Sal James from the International Union of Electricians. How are you today?"

"Fine," he said abruptly. "Whad'ya want?"

"Mr. Batty, we were wondering if you would be interested in donating to our union's relief fund. This fund would be used to support our membership in the event of –"

"Not interested," he said and hung up.

I turned my cell off and then replayed the recording of Bill's voice in the stress analyzer program. I made a copy of the file, and then loaded it into a special voice modeling software that I used. The modeling program analyzed Bill's voice and built an algorithm that could take any other person's speech and simulate it to sound like him. I connected my cell phone to the computer to have my voice run through the modeling program, and then spoofed Bill's cell number into my phone. As a final precaution, I launched a special app that was loaded onto the phone. The application was a distortion filter that would introduce breaks, static, crackling, and the general garble that occurs when someone is going through a weak cell area. It was popular with boyfriends and husbands who didn't want to talk to their significant others when they were late coming home from work and out playing around.

I dialed the number for the Champion Oil Main Crude Unit Control House.

"Main Crude Unit."

"Bill Batty for Nate Walker."

"Who?" The man yelled.

"Bill Batty. I need to talk to Nate Walker."

"Just a minute," he said. "I can hardly hear you."

He barely covered the receiver again and I heard him yell out, "Nate!"

A few moments later, the same man bellowed, "Bill Batty."

"Hold on."

There was a sound of clumsy shuffling as the receiver was handed off. Finally...

"Hi Bill. Whut's up?"

The voice was slow, drawling, and with a southern accent.

"I want to talk to you," I said, hoping the modeling program was working it's magic.

"I can hardly hear you Bill."

"Shitty cell service," I explained.

"Whut?"

"Shitty cell service!" I screamed into the phone.

"Yeah," guess so," he drawled. "Why'd ya call the control room? Why dint'ya call mu cell?"

"New phone and all of the contacts didn't transfer over. Give me your number again."

"Whut?"

"Give me your cell number again!"

He recited it and I wrote it down.

"I want to talk to you," I said finally. "I'll call you tomorrow."

"Whut?"

"I said, 'I'll call you tomorrow!'"

"Okay."

I hung up.

Hello Mr. Walker!

SIXTEEN

I checked the clock and did a quick calculation of the time. It was quarter to eleven and I had to meet Naoko at the restaurant at 1:00. I went online and Yelped local flower shops. I found one not far from the restaurant, and ordered a dozen red roses for pick-up by 12:30.

If I were lucky, I would have about an hour or so left to investigate Nate Walker before I had to take a shower, change, and head out the door. I launched the Emperium website and started digging.

As always, the first info I found on him was just the basic stuff: place of birth, age, education, and social security number. As I suspected from the drawl of his voice, he was from the south, a small town in Oklahoma named McCallister. He was born in 1957 and lived there until he graduated from high school in 1975. Thereafter, he immediately joined the US Army where his MOS was listed as "Motorized Equipment Operator." He moved west to California after finishing his stint for Uncle Sam, and worked a series of menial jobs before finally ending up at Champion. He started in the job of Plant Helper and entered the Plant Operator Training Program three years later. This must have catapulted him into the category of a catch because he married to his wife Helen Sue Walker (nee Jorgenson) shortly thereafter in 1989. The blessed union produced two offspring, a son and a daughter, both of who were now legal adults. I did a quick scan of info on Mrs. Walker, and nothing jumped out at me and grabbed my nose. I shifted gears and went into the financials, as this is where I suspected the pay dirt would be found.

Nate had a steady employment record with Champion which was evidenced by his tax returns. In fact, his income was far higher than the US average and possibly higher than most of his co-workers. This was telling. I checked historic hourly wages for unionized refinery workers and did the math by dividing his income by the number of working hours per year. As I suspected, he worked prodigious amounts of overtime at the plant. The next question was why? And where was it all going?

Mrs. Walker made $58,321 as the Supervisor of Accounts Payable for an HMO, according to her last W-2 form. Add to that the $154,988 that Nate made last year at Champion and they were north of the $200K figure. So much for the income side of the cash-flow sheet. Time to see the outlays. It was not pretty.

The next several pages of data mining produced a picture that told of poor financial decisions, hard money loans, and a climate of desperation. They owned a home in the working class town of Gardena but were heavily leveraged on it, and were as upside down in their equity as a sleeping bat. Their credit card balances were stratospheric, and the bills more often than not, had late fees tacked onto them. No amount of overtime by Nate seemed to stop the hemorrhaging for long. Only twice in the couple's spotty credit history – once in May 2011, and another time in September of the same year - did it appeared that an infusion of cash stemmed the tide, with the balances being paid down in huge chunks – but not for long.

I made a quick note of the dates and sent Marion an e-mail asking if they happened to coincide with any of Rick Harris's "Midas Touch" prognostications about which way the gasoline futures market would swing. It was becoming increasingly likely that Mr. Nathaniel Walker was a prime candidate for the malfeasance at Champion Oil.

Although my instincts told me differently, I looked into the lifestyle of the Walkers. It was far from lavish. Nate drove a 2003 Buick LeSabre and his wife had a 2012 Kia Sonata. The credit card purchases didn't reveal any wild shopping sprees at Nordstroms or Macys by Mrs. Walker, and they owned no boats, RVs, Lear jets or French villas. I turned my attention back to the couple's children as the road to bankruptcy had often been paved by the financial misdeeds of those sprung from the loin.

Of their two children, the oldest, a daughter, had left home to go to college out of state and never returned. She earned an MBA at the University of Wisconsin at Madison and apparently did it all on her own. Employment records showed she worked two jobs while going to school full time. She had a couple of student loans that she paid off within a few years of graduating and was also the recipient of a couple modest scholarships. In all, she was a self-made woman.

After college she relocated to Minneapolis, Minnesota and took a job with General Mills. This was apparently where she met her husband because they both worked there and made good salaries. They owned a home in the city, a cabin up in the northern part of the state, a boat, and both had impressive 401k's.

The younger Walker was a boy who enlisted with the Navy while still in high school. He left for boot camp three weeks after graduating and apparently was still in the service as an aircraft mechanic working on F-18s. He had one loan for a 2012 Chevy Camaro through the Naval Credit Union, and the payments came right out of his pay. There were no indications of other loans, or of any issues with his credit. Other than having an auto loan and money for beer and such, he, like most service members, had few living expenses. Uncle Sam did a good job taking care of his own with "three hots and a cot" and I doubted if the son was feeding at the teat of dear old mother and dad.

I checked the time. It was already 11:50 and I had to get ready to meet Naoko for lunch to patch things up. I took a quick shower, shaved, and was heading out the door when the laptop signaled I had a new e-mail.

It was from Marion and I stood over the computer as I read it. She confirmed that one of the dates of the Walkers' financial rescue was just after Rick, Bill, and company, had managed to sabotage the Champion facility and disrupt the gasoline market. She wasn't sure about the other date, but this was good enough for me. I stepped out the door and headed to the restaurant to meet Nalco. I had one more phone call to make, and I would have to do it in the car on the way over.

SEVENTEEN

The raspy voice on the other end of the phone, roughened from decades of hard drinking and chain smoking, confirmed I had dialed the correct number. Big Tony Scarcetti lived hard and played hard. Besides the usual expression of "live fast and leave a nice looking corpse," he had a couple of other credos he lived by, while attempting to slowly die by nicotine and alcohol suicide. One, any man who goes to bed at night without a woman should hang up his balls. And two, any man who gets up before noon is a sucker. It was 12:05 when I called from the car.

"Hi Tony, John Sharp."

"Jack!" he croaked harshly. "One-Fucking-Eyed Jack! How are you these days kid? Or better yet, what sort of fucking trouble brings you to me?"

"No trouble Tony. Just had a quick question I was hoping you could answer."

"And you had to call this fucking early to ask it?" he chided. He started laughing at his own joke and this triggered a phlegmy, violent coughing jag. It lasted for just a few moments before he reached for his relief.

There was a slight pause as he inhaled on his cigarette. Big Tony also bragged that he only lit one cigarette a day, although he smoked all day long. Upon awakening, he lit the first cigarette of the day with his lighter, lighting every one afterward off of the end of the previous one.

His lungs soothed by the fresh injection of tar, nicotine, and carbon monoxide, the coughing fit subsided and he returned to our conversation.

"So what was it you wanted to know Jack?"

"A guy by the name of Nathaniel Walker. Ever hear of him?"

Another pause, another blessed inhalation of toxins.

"Nathaniel Walker," he repeated slowly. "Nate Walker...also-known-as 'always late-Nate'." Sure I know him Jack, every guy in this town who makes book knows him."

"What does he bet?" I asked. "Sports, football cards, ponies...what?"

"Only the ponies. He says they talk to him sometimes."

"And what do they say?"

"Nothing worth a shit. He owes everybody in LA, and a couple guys in the OC, and usually is scrambling around trying to keep everybody paid off just enough that he doesn't get curb stomped."

There it was. Nate Walker had an equine addiction. And it kept him working overtime and high-stepping to keep from getting his thumbs cut off.

"Can you do me a big favor Tony?" I asked.

"That depends," he said cautiously.

"I need this guy to stay healthy – at least for a while. Can you get the word out to the books you know, asking them to just lay off him for a while. I'm not saying let him off the hook for the bank mind you, but just no leg breaking for a little while. I promise I can make it worth your while."

There was a pause as another long drag was inhaled. Tony was thinking. I wasn't family or a "made" guy by anybody's definition and yet, here I was, asking for a substantial favor usually reserved for those on the inside. Still, I was a stand up guy who could be trusted in Tony's eyes, and I could always be counted on to return the favor if need be.

"Okay." He said finally. "You got it Jack. I'll put the word out and keep him from becoming fish-food, but only for so long. These guys are businessmen you know."

"I understand Tony, and I appreciate it. Give me a month. And if I can't get something going by then, I'll let you know and you can fire up the wood chipper. Thanks again."

"No problem One Eyed Jack."

"By the way," I said. "Does he ever win?"

This triggered a hearty laugh from Tony that soon erupted into another full-blown coughing fit.

"Are you –" cough, cough "kid-" cough, cough "kidding Ja-" cough, cough "Jack?" cough, cough

"They never" cough, "fucking" cough, cough "win" cough, " Ha...ha...ha..."

He hung up just as a lung was being expelled and I was pulling into a parking space at Beach Cities Flowers. I was beginning to formulate the plan I had told Marion I would come up with. But for the time being, I had a woman to woo back into my life. I stepped into the store just as my phone chimed that I had a text. It was from Naoko.

"Won't be able to make lunch. Sorry."

EIGHTEEN

I stood in front of the counter, staring at the text. A woman came out of a refrigerated room wiping her hands on a dirt stained terry-cloth towel.

"Can I help you?" she asked pleasantly.

"I – I'm not sure. Give me a minute please."

She nodded and began moving some cardboard boxes filled with stems and wilted leaves from behind the counter. I typed in a response.

"K. I understand. How about dinner 2night? What would u like?"

I hit send and stood waiting for a response. It seemed like an eternity. The woman, apparently miffed that I was going to stand there ignoring her, returned to her work in the cooler. Finally...

"Not 2night. Real tired."

That was it, no further explanation given, no rescheduling for tomorrow, no "muaah" or ;-(or

"XOXOXO" just, I'm not going to see you, today or tonight. How about ever again? I wondered.

I started to type out a reply to force the issue and see what was at the bottom of this, but then thought better of it. I took a deep breath, keyed in a quick, "No worries. I understand" and let it go at that. I didn't think I'd gain any ground pushing her and would just wait for things to settle down.

Since I had already paid for my flowers online, I picked them up and then handed them to the first woman I saw on the street, telling her to have a great day.

Even with the satisfaction of knowing I had performed a random act of kindness, my mind was still a jumble with the motivations and machinations of so many different people. I needed to clear my head, and went home to get my bike.

NINETEEN

There would be a shift change that occurred between the operations personnel anytime between 5 and 6:00 p.m. at the Champion Oil Refinery. This was the time that the night shift would arrive, receive a status turnover from the day shift, and the reins would be handed off. Oil refining was a 24 hour a day/365 days a year operation that never missed a beat. Unless of course, someone wanted it to.

I arrived around 4:00 and began a sweep of the parking lot, looking for Nate Walker's car. My thighs were burning as a result of the killer workout I had subjected them to in an attempt to clear my head. I had a nebulous plan for handling the Marion Holtzinger/Bill Batty/Rick Harris/Nate Walker situation, but I couldn't sort out my own relationship issues with my girlfriend.

I found his car shortly after arriving and quickly hacked into the keyless entry system. I parked my car a couple blocks away and walked back to the Champion parking lot. I took up a spot near the exit, under the cover of a shade tree, and began waiting. A few minutes after 5:00, men began to come and go through the turnstiles that led into the plant. Nate Walker came through the turnstile at 5:25 and headed toward his car.

He was a tall, lanky man who looked like he would snap like a twig in a stiff breeze. He was wearing a pair of tan Dickies and a plaid shirt, and his clothes hung on him like a sack on a hat rack. The first thing he did upon exiting the turnstile was to reach into his shirt pocket and pull out a pack of cigarettes. He lit one with a hand that I could see shaking, even from my perch fifty yards away, and stepped quickly toward his car. His head twisted nervously from side to side as he moved, and his watery eyes darted about. He was a man who lived in constant fear of what the next turn might bring and I wouldn't be surprised if he checked for bombs underneath his car before he got in. I leaned further back into the shadows of the tree.

His car started with a puff of smoke, and I could see the door locks retract into the secure position before he began to back out. With so many workers coming and going at once, there was a bottleneck at the parking lot exit. Nate was two cars back when I made my move.

Stepping from the shadows, I walked straight toward the passenger side of his car. I pushed the button on the universal key-fob in my pocket and the door locks magically popped up. I grabbed the door handle and climbed in before he had a chance to hit the "lock" button again.

"Start driving," I said flatly. "Southbound on Crenshaw."

He didn't say anything, but I saw the Adam's apple bob in his bony neck as he swallowed.

We were barely on our way when he began to speak.

"I – I got the money comin," he muttered shakily. "Got me thirty-some hours of overtime on this pay-"

I silenced him by reaching into the ashtray and grabbing his lit cigarette. He recoiled back in his seat as if I was going to extinguish it in his eye. He might have had just such a pleasant experience before. I rolled my window down a few inches and tossed the butt out. I had a good sense to dump the whole overflowing ashtray, the way the car reeked. On the seat between us was a folded Racing Form. It had red circles around the names of a couple of horses that probably were in a glue bottle by now.

"Turn right at the next street," I said.

He slowed and we turned onto an industrial street filled with drab buildings with company names no one had ever heard of. There were just a few cars left in some of the parking lots, and any employees remaining were heading home for the day and going in the opposite direction.

At the end of the block was a shuttered building with a long driveway that went around to the rear. The asphalt had weeds and crab grass growing up through cracks. A giant scrawl of boastful graffiti on one wall of the decrepit building claimed that this was the territory of the NST gang.

I told Nate Walker to pull in and follow the driveway around to the back. His hands began to shake on the steering wheel so violently it gyrated. He had the sickening feeling he was about to say goodbye to a part of his anatomy. I could understand this feeling and sympathized with him a bit. After all, I had lost a body part of my own by messing with the wrong people. Such were the stakes in these games.

"Park here," I said.

He slowed to a stop and pulled the selector into "Park." I switched off the ignition and dropped the keys onto the stained floor mat at my feet. There were a couple of other crumpled Racing Forms and some empty cigarette packs on the floor.

I took a good look at him now that we were parked. He had a drawn, leathery face creased with worry lines. His eyes were bloodshot and his lips were dry and cracked. His teeth were yellowed from nicotine, one was missing and another was chipped. I wondered which bet he had tried to welch on.

"Like I said," he began. "The money's coming. I'll have you another fifteen hunred – "

"I'm not here to talk about gambling debts Mr. Walker," I said. "I'm here to talk about terrorism, and about your role in the Champion Oil accidental shutdowns."

"Whut?" He said, trying his best to sound incredulous.

I pulled out an ID and flashed it toward him very officially, letting him also see the holstered sidearm under my jacket.

"Ed Reader, Department of Homeland Security," I recited rapidly. "Mr. Nathaniel Howard Walker, you're under investigation for acts of terrorism against a facility deemed vital to US interests; namely, the Champion Oil Refinery. Your participation in these acts can and will be taken as hostile threats to the security of our nation and to its allies, and are therefore considered acts of treason against the United States of America. Do I make myself clear Mr. Walker?"

"I didn't do nothin."

I replaced my wallet, removed my sunglasses, and turned towards him. He gasped so loud I thought he was going to have a heart attack.

I once had a mark in the entertainment industry that worked designing special effects prosthetics for movies and such. There was nothing illegal or immoral about that, but he also ran a profitable little side business, bootlegging first run films before they'd even hit the big screen. Besides keeping me in new DVDs, along with some extra cash, I also had him design and build a special ocular for me. It was similar to one he had done for a sci-fi film that never got made and it had bright blue LED's arraigned in a starburst pattern. The lights pulsed and oscillated rhythmically, or a remote device in the user's pocket could control it. It fit neatly into my empty left eye socket. I originally had him make it for me as part of a costume for Halloween parties, but hadn't had a chance to use it until now.

"Mr. Walker," I continued in my staccato recital, "The United States Government has made it possible for me to automatically detect any sort of falsehoods, misrepresentations, or outright lies you intend to present."

I pointed to my pulsing eyeball.

"The cobalt lasers in this device can detect the slightest variations in your facial muscles and can measure them down to the billionth of an inch. If you try to lie to me – even slightly – it will pick up tremors in your skin that you are not even aware of."

He gasped again and leaned away from me.

"Just to show you that it works, I want you to tell me a lie. How old are you Mr. Walker? Lie to me."

"Ummm...Ummm – Thirty."

The LED's in the ocular were synched to a small voice stress analyzer in my pocket. If Nate Walker came clean and told the truth, the device would remain idle and the LED's would stay stable. If he lied, as he was doing now, the analyzer would vibrate and the LED's would brighten and oscillate.

I could feel the analyzer vibrate and saw the reflection of blue light on his haggard face brighten and begin to dance around wildly.

His fear turned to panic and he reached for the door handle to get out, I grabbed him roughly and pulled him back.

"Sit down Mr. Walker. We're not finished here."

I pointed upward. "As we speak, a communications satellite in geo-synchronous orbit is beaming video of you, and our conversation, to a secret government location where it is being recorded and will be used against you at a military tribunal, should you choose not to co-operate.

That is, of course, if you decide not to cooperate and, if the government chooses to give you a trial should you do so. There are, as you might imagine, other methods they may want to use. Do you understand the implications of our conversation Mr. Walker?"

"Yeeesss sir," he stammered. His hands were shaking uncontrollably.

"And do you agree to cooperate fully with the United States Government?"

He nodded.

"Say it."

"Yes sir."

"Very well. Do you know Bill Batty?" I asked.

"I'm not sure. I –"

Inside my pocket the analyzer vibrated and I could see the blue glow inside the car brighten again and dance around indicating a lie. Nate Walker shuddered.

"I mean, yes…yes sir; I know him."

That's better Mr. Walker. And Bill Batty had you perform sabotage at the Champion Oil Refinery, didn't he?"

He took a deep breath and lowered his head somewhat. A barely audible "yes sir," escaped his lips.

"Louder Mr. Walker," I said. "So they can hear you at headquarters."

"Yes sir," he said louder.

"Which unit was it Mr. Walker?"

"The Main Crude Unit. That's the biggest unit in the plant."

"And how did you perform this sabotage Mr. Walker? Certainly this unit has monitoring devices. How could you get away with it?"

He thought for a while before answering. Like the best trap, there was no way out.

"Old valves," he drawled finally. "Old solenoid valves."

When he said this, it came out as "sulernode vavs."

"And what did you do with these valves Mr. Walker? How did these 'solenoid' valves result in the shutdown of Champion's Main Crude Unit?"

"I jus whacked um," he said easily." All you gots to do is whack um hard enough and they trip off. Then the unit goes down. Ain't no tattle-tale indication of a button being pushed or anything, so nobody knows how it happened."

I was curious how a weakness in the plant's system could have been discovered and exploited undetected.

"And where did you learn about this Mr. Walker – about "whacking the valves" - to make the plant go down?"

"Bill Batty," he said. "Back when Bill was our Chief Union Steward, we was having some trouble with the company not givin us our due with our new contract. Bill showed me an a couple other Operators how to do it. He said if we dun't get our new contract then we should make the company pay by bringin down the unit."

"And how long ago was this Mr. Walker?"

Nate thought for a while before answering. The stress analyzer remained still, and the blue light in the car remained at a low, steady pulse.

"Bout ten years or so I suspect."

"Did you ever have to do it, or did the contract get settled?"

"Company finally settled, an we dint have to do it."

"And where are these other Operators now, the ones who know about "whacking the valves" to shut down the plant down?"

"Gone. They was older fellas. They both retired and one guy jus passed away a couple years ago."

"Does anyone else know about these valves and what they could do Mr. Walker? This is very important to our investigation."

"I dunt think so. I never told no one. Don't need to borrow any more trouble."

An understatement for sure. Nate Walker had a daily supply of trouble without cultivating any more.

"And so let me get this straight Mr. Walker: You or any other operator never had cause to "whack the valves" and shut down the plant during a labor dispute."

"Yes sir. That's correct."

No vibration, no change in light pulse.

"Until Bill had you do it those two other times, correct? Once in May of 2011 and once again in September, correct?"

His head drooped slightly in shame. "Yes sir," he said. "But I needed me the money. Those guys were gonna – "

"Those guys are nothing compared to my guys Mr. Walker! I can assure you of that! The government knows all about the men that you owe money to. In fact, you will be given a reprieve of sorts, if you cooperate with us."

"A whut?"

"A reprieve. The government can make sure those men don't bother you while you're cooperating with us. Your debts to them will not be relieved outright, and you will still have to pay them back eventually, but they will not bother or threaten you, as long as you cooperate with us. Would you like to cooperate with the United States Government, Mr. Walker?"

"Yeah," he cried enthusiastically. "Hell yes. What do I gotta do?"

"In a short time, Mr. Batty will contact you and ask you to perform the same sort of sabotage you carried out before. You will agree to cooperate with him, and you will receive further instructions from us at that point. You will not speak to anyone: Bill, your wife, your supervisor, the local police – anyone, about our conversation today and what you are going to do. Do you understand me Mr. Walker?"

"Yessir."

"Good. Now hand me your cell phone."

* * *

By six o'clock Nate Walker was dropping me back off a couple of blocks away from the refinery. After I saw his taillights disappear down the boulevard, I started walking slowly back to my car.

I had reprogrammed his cell phone so that any calls he made or received would instantly be routed through my own phone as a three-way call. I could listen in silently, or I could join the conversation, or terminate the call completely. I also had the ability to shut his phone off whenever

I wanted to as well as eavesdrop on any conversations that took place around it whether the phone was switched on or not. Besides this, every phone call, voice message, text or instant message would be automatically recorded in a data server account I kept out on the cloud. Lastly, I activated the GPS tracker in his phone so that it would broadcast at all times where my little stooge was.

I admonished him not to let the phone out of his sight, even when he went to the bathroom or slept, and that I would occasionally send him a text message asking him to verify his presence by deleting the message. If I didn't see him delete the message within five minutes, I would assume he was no longer cooperating with the United States Government and would be considered a hostile enemy of the State. I didn't need to tell him what would happen to him. I just let his imagination run away with itself.

I was almost to my car when I remembered the prosthetic eye. I removed the artifice from my socket and held it in my hand, it's blue iris staring up at me and pulsing benignly. I started to laugh hysterically at the sight of it.

"One Eyed Jack," I said to myself. "You are friggen nuts!"

TWENTY

I spent the next several days shadowing Rick Harris and cataloging his every move. It was the boring, monotonous part of my job that I loathed, but it was necessary. I tried to stay busy and productive during the long hours of these stakeouts by taking care of business, both professional and personal. I handled e-mails, sent friendly reminders to the marks that were behind in their payments, and kept tabs on my new friend Nate Walker. I eavesdropped on the few calls that he made and received, and sent a couple of text messages to him to make sure he was behaving and not leaving his phone. He promptly deleted the messages exactly as I had instructed.

I also sent some texts and left voice messages for Naoko. She responded only to the texts, and not with much enthusiasm. Several times I invited her for dinner and to stay over, and she always replied that she would have to get back to me. Up until now, she hadn't. When I was through with this project, I resolved to take some time off and patch things up with her – if there was anything left to patch up. For now, I had a nefarious futures trader to ensnare in my trap.

Like most people, Rick Harris had a routine that didn't vary much. He left his condo in Belmont Shores about 7:00 a.m. every morning, stopped at a nearby Starbucks to pick up a latte, and then headed into work. His office was located on the top floor of an eight story building in downtown Long Beach on Ocean Avenue, and he parked his BMW in the building's underground parking structure. Not wanting to miss out on any of the action, should a war erupt in the Persian Gulf, or our Commander In Chief catch a bullet, he didn't leave the building at lunchtime and apparently ate at his desk. Marion later confirmed this in response to an e-mail I sent to her, and added that traders called this "commando" style.

He left work every day at about 5:00 p.m. and headed over to a gym a couple of miles away where he took spin and Pilates classes. The gym was located in a less than desirable part of town, and had a large outdoor parking lot in the rear of the building with the main entrance facing out toward it. I could see perfectly down into it from the top deck of a four story parking structure that abutted the rear of the lot. There was no security guard on duty, but two security cameras looked out onto the parking lot from above the entrance. I knew the brand and they were low-resolution cheapies that provided the naive gym members with a false sense of security and not much else. The parking lot was mostly full by the time Rick arrived, and he normally had to park toward the back of the lot and away from the entrance. The overhead lights of the lot were an older style and put out just barely enough illumination to find your car. Several of the bulbs at the back of the lot where he had to park were out, so it was even darker there. The setup was perfect.

For operations like this, I had to rely on outside help. Tequan Sheshawn Tower was a huge African American from nearby South LA. He had once been drafted into the NFL as a middle linebacker, but only lasted a season and a half before being cut and disappearing into the obscurity of short-lived pro athletic careers. Since then, he stayed busy by acting as an enforcer and muscle for the sundry loan sharks, drug dealers, and pimps of the area. He was huge, intimidating, and wasn't afraid to use violence when necessary. For this job he had brought along an associate, another African American who looked like a crack addict that would do anything to score enough money to get his next hit. I didn't know his name and didn't want to. I had instructed both of them what I wanted done, and told them not to resort to violence. If things got dicey, they were to simply abort the mission and they would still get paid.

In contrast to the two of them was John Fallon. Lily white, clean cut, and fit. He was an aspiring actor that had done a couple of bit parts in movies, as well as a bunch of infomercials for fitness supplements and products. At 3:00 a.m. across America you could switch on the TV and see him raving about how he had lost so much weight, or gotten so fit by using this or that product. In between waiting for the calls from Steven

Spielberg or James Cameron that would never come, he did occasional side jobs for me to help pay the rent. He stood next to me on the upper deck of the parking structure as we waited.

It was a little after five-thirty when we saw Rick Harris' shiny black BMW swing into the parking lot of the gym and begin prowling for spaces. I made a call to Tequan.

"He just pulled in," I said when he answered. "No spots in the front, he'll have to go to the back."

I heard a deep voice boom in my earpiece.

"Got it."

Rick Harris drove down one lane near the front of the lot looking for an empty spot before realizing it was fruitless and headed toward the back. He finally found a spot in the second from the last row and got out, swinging his gym bag onto his shoulder as he shut the car door. He aimed the key fob towards his car and the lights flashed. Tequan and Crackhead made their move quickly and cornered him between a row of cars.

In less than ten seconds it was over, with Rick Harris easily giving up his wallet, watch, and cell phone to the two menacing thugs. Tequan and Crackhead took the booty and sprinted out of the parking lot. Rick Harris, frazzled and shaking, slumped over next to an SUV and put his hands on his knees to steady himself. He took a couple of deep breaths and, recomposed, did what he should have done as soon as they cornered him; he hit the "panic" button on his key fob and the BMW erupted into an irritating cycle of wailing horn bleats and flashing lights.

Tequan and Crackhead arrived back on the top deck of the parking structure just a few moments later, breathless and sweaty. Rick had settled down enough by this time and was heading toward the gym to report the crime and call the police.

"Here you go," Tequan said as he handed Rick's phone to me.

I retrieved two envelopes with five hundred dollars apiece in them from inside my jacket and handed one to each of them. Tequan slipped his into his jacket nonchalantly without looking at it. Crackhead tore his open like he was a starving man that I had just given a bag of pretzels to.

"Thanks man," Tequan said. "This'll help. Motherfucker only got twenty-seven bucks in his wallet. Don't nobody carry cash these days?"

As much as they wanted to take Rick's BMW to strip it, they were instructed to leave the keys with him and only take his wallet, watch, and cell phone. They could do what they wanted with the rest, I only wanted the phone.

I plugged it into my laptop just as the wailing from the BMW stopped.

"He's inside the gym," John the actor announced.

I nodded and went to work, reprogramming it with the same stealthy apps I had installed on Nate Walker's phone. Sated with their cash, a watch they could hock, and credit card numbers they could sell, Tequan and Crackhead drifted off and disappeared into the shadows as John and I kept an eye on the gym.

A minute later a police cruiser pulled up to the entrance just as I handed the phone to John.

"It's show time," I said. "Break a leg."

He jerked a thumb in the direction Tequan and Crackhead had disappeared into.

"Glad you didn't use that expression on those other guys," he quipped, "They would take it literally."

I chuckled and then said, "Just do your job - and don't over-act."

"Never," he said as he jogged off.

He was wearing a stylish powder blue sweatsuit, had a matching gym bag, and looked like a thousand other California fitness freaks as he trotted up to the entrance of the gym. He made a sham gesture of delight at the police cruiser outside as he stepped inside the entrance to the gym. At this point, all I could do was wait and hope that it all went down as planned.

The story would go that he was jogging over to the gym to try it out as he was getting dissatisfied with his regular health club. On the way, he spotted a cell phone that had been dropped on the sidewalk. He picked up the phone with the intent of calling the police to turn it in as soon as got to the gym. How fortuitous was this that the police were already there? Even more amazing was the fact that the owner was there and could identify it on the spot!

There would be some questions directed to John about how he found the phone, and where and, "what were you coming to the gym for?" And these would be asked several times by the police and in many different forms. But as an actor, John Fallon was a consummate liar who convinced his audience that he was who he said he was, felt what he said he felt, and did what he said he had done.

About ten minutes after they had arrived, I watched the two policemen exit the gym and drive away. They hadn't walked out the scene of the crime with Rick, nor taken any pictures. All they did was take a report to turn in to headquarters knowing that the chances were slim that they would ever catch the perpetrators.

My phone beeped that I had a text. It was from John.

"All good. They bought story. Rick has phone. 2 many prints 2 dust & no calls made other than his. Going 2 do my work out. I like this place."

With nothing left to do, I got in my car and headed home. I kept checking my phone for messages from Naoko, but there were none. As I got closer to home my phone chimed the ring-tone that told me Rick Harris was making a phone call. I looked at the display and saw that it was an 800 number. I watched as he keyed though the menu and then listened in as he spoke to a sympathetic associate at Chase Card Services informing her that his credit card had been stolen.

I didn't need to hear any more tonight and disconnected just as I was pulling into the parking space at my condo. The servers would pick up any activity and I could review it all tomorrow. It had been a long, crazy week and right now I needed a hot shower, a cold beer, and a dynamite relationship counselor.

I stuck the key into the deadbolt lock on my front door and went to turn it. There was no resistance. The deadbolt was already unlocked.

Quietly, I tried the doorknob and it turned easily. Someone was in my apartment.

I quietly set my laptop case down on the landing and unzipped it. Next to the computer was my Taser gun. I pulled it out, stepped to the side, and opened the door rapidly. I went in, sweeping the weapon in an arc. I froze on the unexpected guest standing in the middle of my living room.

TWENTY-ONE

She stood there motionless as I slowly lowered the gun.

"Sorry Jack," Naoko said apologetically. "I just let myself in. I needed to get some of my things."

I looked at a tall stack of clothes in her arms.

"Some of them, or all of them?"

She didn't answer, and I turned back to the front door and retrieved my laptop case from outside. I set it and the gun down on the floor, and closed and locked the door.

"Sit down," I said. "We need to talk."

She set her clothes down on the coffee table and took a seat on the couch. I sat down on the couch as well, though not right next to her. We both sat silently for a long time; me staring at her, her staring at her hands and not looking up.

"What the hell is going on Naoko?" I said finally.

She took a deep breath and without looking up said, "I'm thinking of moving back to Hawaii."

"Oh," I said. "Just like that, huh? Were you going to tell me, or was I just going to get a postcard of Diamond Head saying, 'Wish you were here?'"

She shrugged, still staring at her hands. She was rubbing them over and over.

"What about us Naoko?"

She finally looked up, and her voice raised several decibels along with it.

"Yes Jack," she said. "What about 'us?' When are we ever going to get serious?"

"What do you mean?" I protested. "We are serious."

"Serious?" she mocked. "You call this serious? We see each other a couple times a week. We have sex, maybe have dinner together, or catch a movie every once in a while. You won't let me move in. You work crazy hours doing God-knows-what."

She gestured toward the Taser. I had explained several times that the people I investigated for the insurance company could sometimes get agitated to the point of violence. She accepted it, but it had always been a point of contention with her.

"And I never know half of the time where you are, or if I can get in touch with you."

She paused for a brief moment, and looked at me narrowly.

"...Or if you're with somebody else," she added.

"Naoko!" I said, slapping my hands down on my knees. "I told you there's nobody else! Why would I stray? You give me everything I want."

"I wish I could say the same Jack," she said, and it stung me.

"Like I said, 'you won't let me move in' and every time I bring up the subject of marriage, or kids or, any sort of a commitment, you avoid the subject like the plague."

She glared at me and took a couple of deep breaths through her nose, the nostrils flaring with her ire. I wouldn't have been surprised to see smoke coming from them.

"So what's this about Hawaii?" I asked

She slammed her fist hard down onto the coffee table.

"Damn it Jack!" she bellowed. "This is exactly what I'm talking about. I try to talk about commitment and you change the subject. You're not going to get out of this by dodging it!"

We both took deep breaths, staring at each other like boxers from opposite corners of the ring. The truth was, I had no comeback. She was right. I tried to tap-dance around any talk about commitment. She was getting tired of it, as any woman would. She looked down at her hands again and her voice lowered.

"My parents are getting old," she said slowly. "They're active and in good health now, but that won't last forever. You know that I'm the only one of my family out here and I'd like to be back there to see them through the rest of their years, unless there was something keeping me here; which I can't say that there is right now."

"What about your job here?" I said, trying hard not to sound like I was steering the conversation too far away from us.

"I can get another job Jack. There are plenty of offices back on the island that are looking for a qualified Vet."

"So you've checked?"

She nodded quietly.

"I see."

I stood up and walked around the living room. It seemed incredibly empty at that moment. For a guy who made his living painting people into corners, I didn't like it very much when my back was against the wall.

"I'm on a really crazy case right now," I said. "It should be over in about a month."

I turned to look at her.

"Can you give me a month and then we can see where we're at?"

"I know where we're at Jack. I just don't know where we're going, that's the problem."

I nodded slowly.

She put her hand on the stack of clothes in front of her flattened the one on the top for no reason.

"Okay," she said. "A month. But I don't think we should see each other in the meantime."

"Okay," I said.

She grabbed the stack of clothes, stood and began walking toward the door. She stepped closer to me. I thought that she was going to give me a hug goodbye. Instead, she handed me her key to my condo. It was already off of her ring and on a paper clip.

TWENTY-TWO

While Nate Walker and Rick Harris' cell phones had been rather easy to acquire and hack into, I could not count on such a luxury with Bill Batty. I doubted seriously if he would buy the whole government investigation thing, and would probably call bullshit and lawyer up. He also didn't strike me as the kind of guy who would give up anything to a street thug without a good fight. That left me only one option.

I was stationed in my replacement surveillance vehicle outside of the Peacock Motel in my usual spot watching and waiting, as Marion and Bill were in the room and in flagrante delicto. She was terrified at first of my plan and resisted having any part of it. But I insisted that it was the only way if we were to ever connect the last piece, bring the whole operation down, and get her out from under Bill's control. As it got closer to her scheduled rendezvous with Bill, she realized how much she hated him, and vowed to whatever she had to end the nightmare.

"I don't care what I have to do," she spit. "I'll walk on hot coals to get rid of that bastard!"

Atta girl.

Emboldened or not, she was still nervous as hell and I could see her shaking as she got out of her car to go into the room. They had been in the room for about twenty-five minutes when my phone rang. It was her.

"He just stepped in," she said. "Please hurry."

"Meet me at the door," I said.

I saw the door to their room crack open a few inches and I raced out of the Astro-Van and was at it in just a couple of seconds.

She had told me that when they had their trysts, she always took a shower before continuing on to work. She normally went first, and then Bill showered after her. I had left a spoof text using her son's cell number on her phone with a message to call. When they were post-coital, she was to pick up the phone, read the message, and inform Bill that she had to call her son, and that he should take a shower first. As soon as he stepped into the shower, she was to call me.

When I got to the door, she opened it a few more inches and held out the phone for me in her trembling hand. I could tell by the bareness of her arm and the fact that she had the door barely open that she was probably naked behind it. I didn't want to violate her modesty any more than it had already been, and just stayed on the other side of the door.

Her hand was shaking so much that I had to

grab it to get the cable into the side of the phone.

"Hold onto it," I said. "And try not to shake. You could make the cable come out."

"Okay," she said quietly. Through the opening of the door, I could smell the mustiness of the room drifting out, and I heard the sound of the water running in the shower. I began to load the programs.

I was half way through when Marion unexpectedly sneezed from behind the door. This caused her hand to jerk and the cable came out of the phone.

"Shit!" I muttered under my breath and quickly reattached the cable.

"Sorry," she said.

"It's okay," I reassured her, although I wasn't sure if it was. I had to start the load all over again and I wasn't sure if we had time. I had already told her that no matter where we were, we would abort as soon as we heard the water stop in the shower.

Part of her foot was exposed and visible through the crack in the door, and it tapped nervously on the threadbare carpet as we both waited for what seemed like an eternity.

"Eighty-five percent," I told her. "Thirty seconds left."

The foot tapped faster and I saw her hair fly as she swung her head toward the shower.

"Ten seconds...five..."

The shower stopped and her foot froze mid-tap.

"Done," I said and she jerked the phone before I had a chance to pull the cable out. The cable pulled the phone out of her hand and it dropped onto the concrete walkway outside the door, causing the door to the battery compartment to pop off and scoot a couple of feet away.

"Oh-no!" I heard her cry from behind the door.

I grabbed the phone and stepped over to pick up the cover.

"Hurry Jack!" she pleaded.

I got the cover on the phone and took a quick appraisal of it. It was still switched on and didn't appear damaged. I turned to hand it to her.

This time all modesty left her and she open the door a foot or so, her lithe, nude body exposed to me.

"Here," I said, trying not to stare and handing her the phone.

She grabbed it and quickly closed the door. I headed back to the Van to wait.

*   *   *

Once in the car, I switched on my phone and activated the eavesdrop app I had just installed on Bill's phone. I could now hear what was going on in the room whether or not he had the phone switched on. If Marion was somehow discovered and things got dicey between her and Bill, then I would figure we were screwed anyway and I would go in and bust it up. I had a few things on Bill that I might be able to use to get him to lay off Marion, but it wasn't as much, or as airtight as I was comfortable with. I pulled out my Taser and set it on the seat next to me just to be ready.

I heard the squeak of the bathroom door as it opened and Bill came out.

A second later I heard him say, "Why is my phone upside down?"

"Crap!"

I heard Marion's voice though she was not as clear or as loud as Bill's. She must have been sitting further away from the phone. Still, I could hear the waver in her voice.

"I – I knocked it off the dresser when I went to move my purse. Sorry. I didn't scratch it, did I?"

I heard a muffled, rubbing sound as Bill must have picked up the phone to examine it.

"You know what I think," Bill said.

My heart stopped, as I knew Marion's did just one hundred feet away. There was no sound from Bill or from her for what seemed like a long time.

"I think I just may want one for the road before I take off. Get on your knees over here and take care of big Bill."

My teeth clenched and I reached over to grab the Taser. I waited for a response from Marion but there was none, no refusal, no pleading, just quiet resignation.

Before long, I heard groans of pleasure coming from Bill. I gripped the Taser even harder and it took all of my resolve to not go break the door down, immobilize him with it, and then squeeze his fleshy neck in my hands until he was dead. God, how I couldn't wait to fry his miserable ass!

The moans ended thankfully just a minute or two later with a loud guttural grunt. A few seconds later I heard him as he moved around the room getting dressed: a zipper being pulled up, a belt buckle jingling, and then finally, the sound of a door being open.

"Same time in two weeks," he said before stepping out of the door and into the bright sunshine. He was smirking his self-satisfied grin as he climbed into his pickup truck before pulling out of the space. As soon as I saw his truck disappear out the driveway of the motel, I called Marion.

"Are you ok?" I asked as soon as she answered.

"Please come in here."

TWENTY-THREE

Chivalrous gentleman that he was, Bill Batty had not bothered to lock the door when he left. I knocked gently and heard a faint, "Come in," from the other side. I stepped into the room and saw that it was as tacky as any I had seen; stained and threadbare carpeting, walls that needed painting, a few crappy pictures hanging crookedly on the wall, and a large sign that loudly warned against smoking in the rooms. There were two queen-sized beds with floral print bedspreads that were so thin they could double as coffee filters. One bed was still made up and Marion's clothes were laid out on it neatly, as if by a valet. She was sitting on the end of the other bed, which was rumpled from the recent activity. She was stark naked and her hair was mussed. Her hands were clasped together in her lap gripping her cell phone and she sat with her shoulders pulled in like a person who was cold and shivering. She stared down at her hands silently. I closed the door and cautiously approached her.

Her shoulders began to shudder and I heard muffled sobs escape her. I sat down next to her and put my arm around her. I pulled her close and she began to wail.

"I hate him!" she said. "God, I hate him!"

"I know, " I said. "I know. Don't worry Marion, we'll get him."

Her head jerked up from the crook of my shoulder and she looked at me with reddened, desperate eyes. Her mascara was running and there was some other liquid on her cheek. I thought briefly of wiping it off with the back of my hand, but didn't want to call attention to it.

"Tell me Jack," she said in a pleading tone. "Tell me this is the last time I'll have to fuck that bastard!"

"It's the last time Marion," I said. "I promise you. Thanks to what you did today, the foundation is set. Now we'll just set the trap."

She let a long breath escape.

"I – I was so scared," she said. "I guess I didn't pay attention to which way Bill's phone was set down, and he noticed it. I thought he would figure it out and start beating me!"

"He wouldn't have done it Marion. I had his phone on eavesdrop mode and was listening in. I heard the whole thing. If things went south, I would have been in here in a second."

I left it unspoken that I heard what Bill had made her do. I'm not sure if she cared that much or not at this point. She was a defeated woman. She just wanted the nightmare to end.

She stared at me for a long time, her eyes begging for reassurance. Finally, she reached up with her hand and touched my face gently.

"Thank you."

I nodded and then squeezed her shoulder one last time.

"Why don't you take your shower," I said. "I can stay here if you want."

"What about Bill? What if he comes back."

I pulled my phone out and checked the GPS tracker I had activated on his phone. The display showed his present position.

"He's three miles away already, and heading further away from us. He won't come back. Even if he did, I'd see it."

She nodded and pulled away.

"Okay," she said. "I'd appreciate it if you could stay here while I take my shower. I feel pretty vulnerable right now."

"I understand."

I continued to monitor Bill's position while Marion showered. As I guessed, he was sated and had no reason to return. Once he started the climb up the hill on the Palos Verdes Peninsula towards his home, I switched the unit off. Marion came out of the bathroom fully dressed. She looked okay but I could tell she was still reeling from her ordeal.

"Do you have time for a cup of coffee?" I said.

She looked at her watch, thought about it, and said, "No...But I'd like to get one anyway."

* * *

We agreed that we should leave Marion's car at the Peacock Motel and take mine to get the coffee. I felt that she might not be in the best condition to drive, and after she had a chance to settle down and recover, she would be in better form.

It was operating under this skewed assumption, that I felt completely idiotic when I pulled right out in front of a car as we exited the driveway of the Peacock. I wasn't used to driving with anyone else in the car and was distracted enough that I forgot to turn my head completely before entering the flow of traffic. Without the aid of my left eye, my field of vision was compromised and I nearly caused an accident. The driver of the other car had to slam on her brakes and swerve to avoid colliding with us. After she recovered, she roared up next to me and gave me a long blast on her horn. I turned to look at her and mouthed the words "I'm sorry."

This caused her to lay off the horn, but not before giving me a queer look. I had not put my sunglasses on, and my left eye was covered with the patch. She did a quick double take before speeding up to pass us. People either stared with perverse curiosity at me, or recoiled in disgust. I was used to it.

TWENTY-FOUR

Like any area, the South Bay of Los Angeles had its share of chain and independent "hipster" coffee joints. Rather than endure the cacophony of endless one-sided cell phone conversations and the tap-tap of laptop keyboards, I settled for an old fashioned family restaurant that still served artery clogging eats, and catered to an older, quieter crowd. Since it was Tuesday morning, the place was crowded with blue-hairs stalking the $3.99 breakfast special. Marion and I found a nice booth toward the rear of the restaurant and settled in over our cups of steaming brew. I insisted that the waitress leave menus as I thought it might do her some good to get something on her stomach. She insisted she was fine and had no appetite, but when the server returned a few minutes later, I ordered us each a freshly baked muffin and told her it was fine if she didn't eat it. A few minutes later, her resolve weakened and she began picking at the top and placing small chunks into her mouth.

"Talk to me Jack," she said.

"About what?"

"Anything. Tell me anything just to get my mind off of this shit. Tell me about where you grew up, your family…anything except 'the foundation' we just laid, or 'the trap' we're going to set."

I considered her request for a long time. For a guy who knew everybody else's lives and secrets, I was terribly reticent to reveal much about myself. This was, of course, another one of Naoko's many complaints about me. But then again, a brutal Neanderthal wasn't using Naoko as a concubine.

"My dad was in the military," I said. "Army. We moved around a lot – base to base. I was never in one place for more than two years."

Without taking her eyes off me, she tore off another piece of muffin and ate it.

"Are your parents still alive?"

"No. My mom died of cancer when I was eleven. My dad re-married but I never liked his new wife, I guess that's pretty common. And when he died, I broke off any contact with his widow."

"Siblings?"

"No. I was an only child – an Army brat of one."

She took a long sip of her coffee and considered this. She could probably imagine the loneliness of being an only child and being schlepped around from base to base, never staying long enough to make any permanent friends.

The waitress came by and topped off our cups. I blew across the top of mine and took a sip. Marion surprised me with her next question.

"Can I ask you how you lost your eye?" she said.

I thought about it for a moment before deciding to tell her. It wasn't a very pleasant story, but then again, neither was my childhood.

"Are you sure you want to hear about it? It's pretty ugly."

She nodded. "Yes. I don't know if I'm just curious, or if it's the 'misery loves company' part of me that would feel better knowing someone else was suffering."

"Sorry," she quickly added. "I guess that doesn't sound very nice."

"Don't worry about it Marion. You've been through hell. It's understandable."

I took another sip of my coffee as well as a deep breath. I tried not to ever think about the incident.

"It happened about six years ago," I began. "I was doing my blackmail thing and had found a wealthy Beverly Hills plastic surgeon I thought I could lean on. He had a nice house, trophy wife, cars, a yacht – he also liked to have sex with male prostitutes. I figured he would be easy mark. He had a lot to lose."

I took a sip of coffee, noticing that I was starting to get the jitters. I wasn't sure if it was from the caffeine or from re-telling my story.

"What I didn't know was that this doctor also was doing some re-constructive work for a Russian mobster – essentially trying to change the guy's appearance so he could live his life out in the open. The mobster was in the US and probably on the run from everybody from the Feds to his enemies' back home. And what the mobster didn't need was a distraction like me while the doctor was taking a scalpel to his face. So he had the doctor take it to mine instead – specifically my left eye."

She shuddered, and her coffee sloshed back and forth in her cup.

"You mean, the doctor removed your eye?"

I nodded.

"Argh! What did you do then? Did you get revenge against them?"

"No."

"Why not?"

"I tried to find out who the Mafioso was, but I could never track him down."

"You?" she said incredulously. "I thought you were an expert at this sort of thing."

I nodded. "I know, it sounds crazy. But think about it; this guy had managed to evade The FBI, The Justice Department, Interpol and God knows who else. How could I, with my measly resources, expect to find him? My targets are ordinary folks; Horny soccer moms and blue-collar lugs who think they can pull a scam because they heard about it from a buddy in a bar. I'm just small potatoes. This guy is in the big leagues. And as much as I wanted to, I couldn't touch the doctor, because they'd kill me the next time."

She stared at me. "Do you think the doctor is still working on him?"

"The doctor died about four years ago in an auto accident. I always thought that it might be due to foul play. I don't know how far along the doctor had been with the re-construction, but two years might have been the time it took to complete all the operations on the mobster and have him heal up. I couldn't prove any of this of course, and there was no way I was running to the authorities with my suspicions."

"What about the mobster?" Marion asked. "Do you think he's still around?"

I raised the coffee cup to my mouth and then set it down without taking another sip.

"I don't know. He could be alive or dead, or living in the Cayman Islands for all I know. I gave up trying to find him, and I hope he forgot all about me."

She looked at her watch. "I really have to get going," she said, sliding across her seat in the booth.

I got out as well and we hugged goodbye. It was nice and I found myself wanting to hold onto her. Whether it was to comfort her or me, I couldn't determine.

"Thank you Jack," she said, looking into my eyes. "For the coffee, and for everything. You're giving me my life back."

"You're welcome Marion."

We uncoupled, and headed back out to my car.

TWENTY-FIVE

"Good morning," the woman behind the desk chirped pleasantly. "May I help you?"

It was nice office, clean and modern. Decorated only in black and white, with shades of gray. I didn't know if it there was a certain subtle message my brain was supposed to pick up on, or if it was simply the result of a limited palette.

"Herr Gustav Heikle to see Rick Harris."

She was 45 to 50 years old, conservatively dressed, and had a reserved, professional demeanor. Try as she might, she could not conceal a sudden shift in her attention when I gave her my name. She had obviously been told I was big news.

"Yes Mr. Heikle," she said brightly. "I'll tell Mr. Harris that you're here. Is there anything I can get for you; coffee, water?"

"No thank you," I said in a thick German accent before adding, "...and it's 'Herr Heikle,' Madame."

"Oh I'm sorry Herr Heikle," she apologized, blushing slightly. "Force of habit I guess. I'll let Mr. Harris know that you're here. Just let me know if there is anything you need."

I nodded and watched her as she picked up the handset on her phone and pressed a button. She was Marion's replacement and had joined Zeus Investments shortly after Marion had left. As per my general practice, I had done a cursory search on her. There was nothing of note; she was innocent, as Marion had been. The real scoundrel was in the next room.

"Mr. Harris," she said into her handset. "Herr Heikle is here to see you."

There was a slight pause and she hung up.

"Mr. Harris will see you shortly," she said to me. "Please have a seat."

She motioned to a gray leather sofa on the opposite wall.

I nodded and took a seat, knowing full well that Rick Harris could have dropped whatever he was doing to see me. He was trying hard not to appear too anxious, even to the man sitting in his reception area who could change his life forever.

I carefully straightened the crease on my pants using both of my hands and stared directly ahead, not at the Receptionist, but through her. My face was expressionless, icy, and I sat ramrod straight, barely moving a muscle. I was a patient man and could wait an eternity for the right opportunity.

Five minutes passed before the Receptionist's phone rang. She answered it, listened, and then hung up.

"Mr. Harris will see you now," she said, and stood to open the door to his office.

I rose slowly and walked across the floor of the reception area with measured steps. I entered the office and the door closed silently behind me. Rick Harris rose from behind his desk and proffered a big hand.

"Herr Heikle," he beamed. "A pleasure to meet you."

I nodded and shook his hand with a medium grip, and only briefly. I wasn't interested in the silly protocols and customs of business. They were time wasters and the world had to be conquered.

"Please sit down, Herr Heikle," Rick said, gesturing to a set of modern leather chairs opposite his desk. "Is there anything we can get for you; coffee, tea, a water?"

"Nothing please," I said taking a seat in one of the chairs. I took a very slow, deliberate look around his office. It was about twenty by twenty, modern and uncluttered. One wall was entirely floor to ceiling windows, and looked out to the north over the City of Long Beach. In the distance, I could see several of the elevated flare stacks of an oil refinery in the City of Carson. Any disruptions to the refinery's operations would cause one of the stacks to emit an enormous flame like a giant blowtorch. From Rick Harris' perch, he would be one of the first to know, and hopefully capitalize on the misfortunes of others.

Herr Heikle would have been impressed with the no nonsense business sense of Rick Harris, but would give none of this away. I kept my expression icily neutral before settling my gaze back on him.

He seemed larger than he had appeared when I watched him get shaken down by my two thugs. But then, anyone would seem small compared to them. He was dressed nicely in a white long sleeved shirt with a dark blue tie. He wore no jacket, and his shirtsleeves were rolled up to the elbows. He began rolling them down as soon as we shook hands. I wondered if it was all theatrics and if he had rolled them up just as soon as he heard I had arrived - the tireless businessman, hard at work for his clients.

I straightened the creases on my pant legs once again, and I could tell by the way Rick looked at me, that I was being studied as well. I was dressed in a jet-black Valentino suit in a sharp European cut. Beneath this was a white dress shirt with French cuffs, and a plain black silk tie that completed the ensemble. I wore no jewelry other than a Tag Heuer Carrera watch and brushed nickel cufflinks. There was no bling with this client, just business.

"Mr. Harris," I began. "As I stated when I spoke to your Receptionist, I represent a European investment group that is interested in moving some of their capital into the commodities markets."

"Absolutely Herr Heikle," Rick said enthusiastically, pulling a yellow legal pad toward him and beginning to jot down notes. "And that's where we at Zeus Investments can help. Were you looking to set up an account today?"

Moving in for the close already, I thought. Not so fast Ricky baby; I'm gonna make you work for it. I ignored his heady solicitation and moved on.

"As I'm sure you're aware Mr. Harris, the European markets have been in turmoil for some time. The Euro has been a disaster, and no one is quite sure where the markets will settle."

"Yes, yes," Rick agreed. "Does your investment group have a heavy position in European equities currently?"

It had taken some work, but I had done some "sock-puppetry" by creating a nebulous presence of the group I purported to represent, "FH-1 Capitol" online. Not much could be gleaned from any of the information, other than to suggest that it was a highly secretive group that guarded the identities of its partners, and their investments, vigorously. No one would know who they were or what they invested in, and they sent lackeys like me to play point man for them. Rick Harris would get nothing. My face tightened as I glared at him.

"I'm not here to discuss the position FH-1 Capitol has in other investments Mr. Harris," I said coldly. "Do I make myself clear?"

Rick immediately realized he had crossed the line by being too inquisitive and began to apologize profusely.

"Of course... of course," he said rapidly. "I did not mean to pry and meant no disrespect Herr Heikle. Please accept my apologies."

I kept my gaze on him for a few long moments. Besides the suit and my demeanor, the black Viper snakeskin eye patch I wore had proven itself equally intimidating.

"We have been studying your company for some time Mr. Harris. You are a Series 3 and a CTA, correct?"

"Yes, that is correct."

"And you have no actions or investigations under way by either the CFTC or the NFA?"

"Again, that's correct sir."

I noticed a bit of pride in Rick's response. There had to be a perverse satisfaction in knowing you had manipulated a commodities market not once – but twice, and not been found out, by the two agencies that regulated it.

"What is your current AUM Mr. Harris?

This was the amount of money that Rick managed for other clients. I already knew the answer, but wanted him to state it.

"A little over eleven million dollars."

"...Spread over how many clients?"

"Twenty Four."

I nodded for the first time and sat facing him silently, like I was digesting it all. Finally, I spoke again.

"Mr. Harris, the group I represent is considering a large investment of funds, equal to what you currently manage, in Zeus Limited. If, after a period of time, we are satisfied with our returns, we would be willing to up the ante to approximately five times what you currently manage. Or, to put it more simply, fifty-million dollars."

Across the desk from me, Rick Harris tried to keep his composure, but it was nearly impossible. I saw his Adam's apple bob as he swallowed. Inside his head, I knew he was already crunching the numbers, the "Two and Twenty" as they were referred to. For managing the capital of outside investors, he would receive two percent of the total, strictly as a management fee. He would also receive an additional twenty-percent of any profit he could show for his work. In other words, if he were able to secure the entire $50 million infusion, he would be guaranteed $1 million in fees, plus twenty percent of the profits. It was a dream come true. I thought I saw him stop breathing.

"We do of course have some concerns Mr. Harris," I said gravely.

"Concerns?" he asked, and put the pen to paper to get it all down.

"Yes. Your record has been good, but not spectacularly so."

He started to speak and I cut him off.

"...Except for two months, May and September of 2011 when your performance far exceeded the market."

He stared at me wordlessly, his head barely moving.

"The returns during those two months had to make your investors very happy Mr. Harris."

"Yes they did Herr Heikle."

"Those type of returns would make FH-1 Capital happy as well. It would be the type of returns that would make us want to invest in Zeus."

Rick nodded slowly and I could see the wheels turning in his head.

"We understand of course that the markets are volatile and that no one has a crystal ball, but we would require a longer track record of consistently positive returns with minimal drawdowns in order to invest in your company. Do you understand the needs of FH-1 Capital Mr. Harris?"

"Yes Herr Heikle," he said, swallowing.

I stood up.

"Very well. As long as we understand each other."

* * *

Rick Harris offered to take me to lunch, but I informed him that I had other commitments. I offered that since he was going to lunch, we could share the elevator down to my car, and he readily accepted.

When we arrived at the "B" level of the underground parking garage, any doubt he might have had regarding the legitimacy of my claims of representing one of the largest investment groups in Europe were quickly dashed. Sitting in the "Visitors" section was an immaculate jet-black SL 63 AMG Roadster. I had rented it from a luxury car outfit in Beverly Hills for the day. It was a rare car by European standards, but they were almost non-existent on American roads. It was a pricey ploy, but when Rick Harris saw it and nearly began to drool, I knew the hook was sunk and he couldn't shake it. I could almost see him fantasizing about having one of his own in just a few months, when FH-1 Capital signed on to Zeus Investments.

He shook my hand and headed back towards the elevators. When the door closed, I hit the key fob and the car's lights flashed.

"Nice car."

I turned toward the sound. I hadn't noticed him before, but a hulking man with a shaved head and a serious Foo Manchu mustache was eyeing the car enviously. He was standing at the passenger side door of a silver BMW Eight Series with heavily tinted glass. Another man was in the driver's seat, but I could only make out his silhouette.

"Thanks," I said.

"Sixty-Three Series' right?" Skinhead said. "I hear it's tough to get them in the US."

He knew his cars.

"Took me two years," I said and climbed into the driver's seat.

*   *   *

I was just leaving the parking structure and pulling out onto Ocean Avenue when my phone went off. I thought for a second that it might have been Rick Harris already starting to orchestrate his big score by calling Bill Batty, but the ring tone was wrong. I looked down and was delighted to see who it was.

"Hi baby."

"You asshole!" Naoko screamed.

TWENTY-SIX

"What?" I said incredulously.

"You heard me Jack."

"Naoko, what's this about?"

"You lied to me!" she hissed.

The lunch crowd was just emerging from their caves, and traffic was turning into a bitch on Ocean Avenue. I pulled over into a "No Parking" zone. I needed to concentrate, and put the Roadster into park.

"Naoko," I said calmly, hoping to settle her down. "Can you please tell me what this is about?"

"Lies Jack! That's what this is about!"

I searched my memory, trying to think of a time where I had deceived her.

"Do you remember Sonia?" she asked.

"Sonia? Sonia who?"

"My Assistant...or rather she was my Assistant for a short time. She got pregnant after about six months and had to quit."

I tried to think of who she was, but drew a blank. "Okay," I prompted. "What about her?"

"You met her once at a Christmas party Doctor Stanford threw for the office."

I tried hard to place her, but couldn't.

"I'm sorry Naoko. I don't remember her. What does she have to do with me or with us?"

"Well she remembers you Jack!" Naoko spit. "She spotted you the other day coming out of a motel – with a woman in your car! The other woman Jack! The one that you swore didn't exist! The one you've been fucking while you strung me along for a year and a half! I hate you...you fucking lying bastard!"

Then it dawned on me, the other day, pulling out of the Peacock, Marion in the car, the woman I almost crashed into. Shit! I tried to think fast.

"Naoko," I pleaded, "I...I was on a case with another associate. She...she..."

"Shut up Jack!" Naoko said. "Keep your lies and your bullshit to yourself!"

There was a rapping sound on my window. I turned my head to look over. It was a parking enforcement person.

"Gotta move," the pimply face kid said.

In the meantime, Naoko kept up her rant.

"...gonna give us another chance..."

I held up a hand to try to get the kid off my ass.

"Naoko please..."

But she wasn't listening, and was still in her diatribe.

"...forgot some of my things at your place. Tell the Manager to let me in to get them. I'm leaving work early today and will be there at 1:00 today. I don't want to see you Jack..."

The kid continued to rap on the window.

"Gotta move or it's a ticket." I heard his muffled voice say.

"...ever again!"

Naoko hung up. The phone went dead in my hand.

"Shit!"

The kid was bringing out his ticket-printing device. Without looking, I threw the car into drive and floored it. A loud truck horn blared from behind me. I didn't care; with five hundred-plus horses under the hood, I was at sixty miles an hour in less than three seconds and could outrun anything. Anything that is, but the wrath of a woman scorned.

TWENTY-SEVEN

I drove on the freeway, back up to Beverly Hills Exotic Car Rentals, at a more sedate speed. All of a sudden, everything had slowed down, and there seemed to be no urgency in my life. Without realizing it, over the last year and a half, Naoko had given me some purpose beyond my everyday existence, beyond the hacking into other people's lives to earn my bread.

Once again, in a moment of weakness, I began to consider leaving the game, and taking a regular job with regular hours, regular pay, and benefits. The thought repulsed me. I had left the life once before and it was a disaster.

It was right after I had the run-in with the Russians, and I had gotten scared. I took a job as an insurance fraud investigator. It was easy work for a guy like me. With my nose for scams, I quickly racked up an impressive list of confirmed kills, busting people trying to claim broken necks or damaged lumbars.

I was so good in fact, that my boss, a woman named Melinda Harrigan, began to feel the heat. With my quick rise to the top of the list, I was eclipsing her, and the Head Office was beginning to wonder if maybe I should be the one running things.

She caught wind of this and immediately tried to push me out of the spotlight. She changed my caseload and I saw my numbers slip. I confronted her about this, but she was all denial and protestations. Backed into a corner, I went on the offensive and resorted to my old tricks. It didn't take me long to find some dirt on her.

It was common knowledge in the office that she had spotty luck with men. One relationship after another seemed to sprout, blossom, and then wither rapidly. With middle age approaching, she was becoming desperate to do anything to keep a man ensnared.

His name was Robert Evans, 34, good looking, and athletic. He had slipped and fallen on some spilled orange juice in a supermarket, and was suing the chain, and us, claiming his knee was damaged beyond repair. While reviewing the cases, Melinda had taken notice of him. Before long, she had made contact and they were dating – an egregious violation of company policy, and a terminable offense.

Using the company's own resources, I built a fat dossier on my boss and her illicit affair, and presented her with the evidence to use as leverage. She immediately tried to cut me a deal.

She would give me a raise, a better office, and even allow me the pick of cases, as long as I buried the dirt on her, and let her stay employed. It was a sweetheart deal and everything told me I should have taken it. But I didn't.

The truth was, I hated the routine, the regular hours, the annual reviews, the bullshit office politics. While building my case against my boss, I realized how much I missed the game, the independence, the thrill of discovery. I told her I only wanted two things: a month's severance pay, and perpetual access to the companies search engine, Emperium. She agreed and I was back.

Now I was questioning my life again, but realizing what it would all mean. I would become one more working stiff again, punching a clock, and marching to the beat of someone else's drum. I would get Naoko back – maybe, but at what cost? Would I resent her? Would I feel as if I had cowered and taken the easy route? The Russians had pushed me before, and I had sworn, never again.

I was on Sunset Boulevard, a block away from the car rental place, when my phone went off, bringing me back to the here and now. It was the ring tone for the hacked calls I was monitoring. It was Rick Harris calling Bill Batty. I pulled down a side street and punched the key to listen in. It was already starting.

TWENTY-EIGHT

Rick's call went straight to voice-mail. Rick was unaware of it, but I could see the 'Ignore" button being pressed on Bill's phone. I listened in as Rick Harris made his attempt to mend fences.

"Hey Bill – Rick. I know it's been a long time. Listen, I'd like to talk to you about working together again. I know that there were some sore feelings when we parted, but I think we can work this out. I think you were right Bill. You did some valuable work for me and I wasn't willing to cut you in on the action. Well, I see the error of my ways now, and would like to make it right. Give me a call."

Rick left his phone number – twice, and then hung up. I continued to monitor Bill's phone and saw that he immediately played back the message. Then, a minute later, he re-played it. A rat sniffing the bait.

* * *

After returning the AMG, I retrieved my car from the valet at the rental lot and began driving south toward home. I made a quick call to my condo complex manager, and informed him that my ex-girlfriend would be coming by today after 1:00 to get the rest of her things, and for him to let her in.

"I can't stay to watch her," he told me. "I have a meeting with the owners of the building."

"That's okay," I said. "She can be trusted. I relieve you of any liability."

And with that, a year and a half relationship ended.

* * *

I would have loved to have climbed onto my bike and rode forever, especially after making the call, but I had focused so much of my effort on the Marion thing lately, that I had neglected the rest of my business. Besides that, it would keep me away from home long enough that I didn't risk running into Naoko.

I hit all of my PO Boxes before returning to the condo and found them overflowing with envelopes stuffed with tithing, even Hard Case's was there, and plumper than usual. At least I wouldn't have to resort to enforcer role once again.

It was 3:30 by the time I arrived back at my condo. I popped into the manager's office and he confirmed that yes, Naoko had come by at about one-o'clock.

"She seemed pretty pissed," he said.

I ignored him and went up to my place.

I took a cursory look around when I got in. Nothing looked like it had been disturbed, and there were no angry notes or a giant, "FUCK YOU JACK!" spray painted on the walls. It was as if she had never been there.

I felt grimy and wanted to take a shower before diving back into all of the paperwork I had to catch up on, so I stripped off my fancy duds, and went to the chest of drawers in my bedroom to grab some fresh underwear and a pair of shorts.

I was surprised when I pulled the drawer open and found a stack of Naoko's clothes still there. Had she had a change of mind, or had she simply forgot they were here?

I checked a couple of other drawers and found some more things. I gathered all of them together and set them in a stack in the corner of the kitchen. If she came by again, I wanted them out where she could find them, but not where I would be looking at them all the time.

I debated back and forth as to whether or not I should call her. I decided against it, but sent a text saying that her things were out and on the table in the kitchen. I added that I really wished she would let me talk to her so we could patch things up. I hit send and felt I had about as much of a chance of reconciling things with her as a stick of butter does surviving on the surface of the sun.

A moment later, my phone chimed again. It was Bill calling Nate. I listened in.

"Hullo?"

"Nate, it's Bill. You at work?"

"Yup."

"Can you talk?"

A pause.

"Yeah, I guess."

"Good. I may have another job for you."

Silence. This was the call Nate had been dreading. He was about to be involved in a government sting operation. Finally…

"Nate? You there?" Bill asked.

"Yeah."

"Can you help me out?"

"Yeah. Sure. Same price as last time?"

"Yes, of course. I'm not going to screw you."

Like hell, I thought.

"Good." Bill said. *"I'll let you know if it's going to go down. What's your schedule like?"*

"Working lots."

"Yup."

"Nights?"

"Yup."

"Good. E-mail me your shift schedule."

"kay."

"Good. I'll be in touch," Bill said, before hanging up.

As soon as the call was terminated, I placed a call to Nate.

He answered with a very cautious, "Hullo?"

"Very good Mr. Walker," I said. "Follow along with Mr. Batty as if nothing had happened. Do you understand?"

"Yup."

"Good."

I hung up.

* * *

A day went by and Naoko had not come by or returned my text. Bill Batty finally returned Rick's call though. He acted like he was disinterested in the whole affair, and that he was only doing Rick the courtesy of returning his call. I was in the shower when it happened, but received a text on my phone letting me know some recent activity had occurred. I logged into my server account and replayed the conversation.

"You called?" Bill said nonchalantly.

"Yes. I'll get right to the point Bill. Would you like to work together again?"

"That depends."

"You still have your guy inside Champion?"

"Maybe. Like I said, ' it depends.' Are you going to take the lion's share again and just leave me a couple of crumbs? Do you know what a risk I'm taking Rick? I could go to jail if anyone knew what I had my guy do."

"So could I Bill," Rick reminded him. *"Besides jail, I'd lose my license to trade commodities."*

"I'm listening," Bill said, waiting for Rick to offer first.

"I'll open an account for you Bill," Rick said. *"And I'll put in the first twenty-five grand. You can add to that whatever you want. Either way, I could see us doubling it on the first trade."*

"I want you to put in a hundred grand," Bill countered.

"That's outrageous Bill!"

"So is what I'm doing for you."

They haggled back and forth for a couple of more minutes, until finally settling on Rick putting up the first $50 thousand. Then Rick told Bill about the latest futures contract expiring next Wednesday, and asked him if he could possibly have it done on Monday night. Bill said he would let him know by the end of the day. Rick in turn, promised to fax over the paperwork for Bill's new account to have him sign it. After all the horrible things I had heard today, this was music to my ears.

TWENTY-NINE

Over the next several hours, there were a flurry of phone calls, texts, e-mails, and faxes flying back and forth between the co-conspirators. I was monitoring every bit of the communications, although at this point, it was essentially out of my hands and on autopilot.

My emotions were in a free-fall, as I had not received a text, e-mail, or call from Naoko. Unable to resist any longer, I sent her another text, asking her to please let me know if she had gotten the one regarding her things.

An hour later, she hadn't called and so I called her on her cell. It went straight to voice mail. An hour later, I rinsed and repeated with the same results. Finally, I called her office and pretended like I was a pet owner in distress and asked if I could please speak to her for a second.

"I'm sorry, but Doctor Kobiashi didn't come in today," Julie, the receptionist informed me.

"Julie, it's Jack," I said. "Her boyfriend. Did she call in sick or take a vacation day?"

There was a long pause as she considered giving out any information. Julie and Naoko were friends, and it was likely that Naoko had told her about our problems.

"Well, I don't know Jack," she said cautiously. "I mean she told me the two of you were –"

"Please Julie," I said. "I just want to make sure she's okay."

"So do we."

What do you mean?"

She took a deep breath and exhaled before continuing. "We're kind of worried ourselves Jack. She didn't show up today for work, and she had a lot of procedures scheduled. And she didn't call in; that's not like her. We've had to shift everything around - that's no big deal. What is a big deal is that we can't get hold of her. I know that she was pretty upset about the stuff between the two of you, and everyone needs some time to themselves, but still –"

I hung up before letting her finish, or saying goodbye. I was out the door in a flash, and on the road over to Naoko's. She lived about two miles away in a condo complex in Torrance. It was smaller and older than mine, and had once been an apartment building before the big "California Condo-Conversion" fever had hit in the seventies.

I drove into the underground parking structure. Four stalls were available for visitors, and I pulled into one of them.

I was just switching off the ignition when I saw another car pull in at an angle behind me, blocking me in. It was a silver sedan with tinted windows. I turned to see what was going on just as the passenger door flew open and a large man sprung out. He was the same hulking skinhead I had seen yesterday in the parking structure of Rick Harris' office. He quickly aimed a suppressed Glock in my direction and fired. The glass in my driver's side window exploded into a torrent of pea-sized chunks as the bullet hit the lower left corner. I closed my eyes and felt the shower hit me in the face. Stunned, I began fumbling in the car for my Taser. It didn't matter as a second later I felt the two darts from skinhead's own Taser hit me in the neck. I lost all control of my motor functions and couldn't fight back when a cloth soaked in chloroform was placed over my face. I felt my eye roll up into my head. Then everything went dark.

THIRTY

"He's coming to," I heard a thick voice say. The sound was watery and it echoed in my head. From the darkness, I saw light coming through my eyelids, an opaque orange glow. I opened them to a milky world that was rolling back and forth, like a ship in a storm. I could see vague shapes close by, they appeared like giant buildings. When they came into focus, I could see that they were men, very large men. One was the skinhead who shot at me. The other had dark hair and what appeared to be a goatee. He looked familiar to me, strangely familiar, frightfully familiar! A pail full of ice-cold water hit me in the face.

"Wake up!" the one with goatee yelled.

It came out as "vake up." And I knew as soon as I heard it, that I was in some deep shit. He was one of the Russian thugs that had helped alter my visual acuity six years ago. They must have tracked me down after I left Rick Harris' office. Shit!

Skinhead reached toward my face and ripped the piece of duct tape off my mouth. I struggled to move my arms but it was futile. I was tied down to a chair.

We were in a tiny, dimly lit room. It was cold and damp. I could hear the muffled drone of some equipment running close by, and the place smelled like rotting vegetables. There was only one door to the room that I could see, and it had thick, beefy hinges as if it weighed a ton.

"What the fuck's going on!" I managed to say in a voice that was thick and drowsy.

Skinhead backhanded me and nearly knocked over the chair that I was sitting in. I felt warm blood begin to flow down from my nose and into my mouth. I tasted iron. He reeled up again to hit me, and then another familiar voice called out from behind me.

"Enough!"

Skinhead's arm froze mid wind-up and I felt my pulse begin to race. Suddenly I was six years in the past, in a makeshift operating room in a mansion occupied by a mobster on the run. The last time I had heard this voice it had promised me that I would see "less of the world" after that day. It was a promise that had been kept.

"Mr. Sharp," the voice said. "Pleasure to see you again. How you Americans say, 'long time-no see?'"

I said nothing. I was still foggy, but had enough sense to keep my mouth shut and let him do the talking.

"You have been a busy man, yes Mr. Sharp?" he said.

"Busy enough."

"And you have business with Mr. Rick Harris I see. You must tell me about it, yes?"

"Why should I tell you about it? It's my business. I'm not interfering with you or the Doctor anymore"

Skinhead apparently didn't like my disrespectful tone and backhanded me again.

But I was either sweating or bleeding so much, that his hand glanced off of my face fairly easily. He didn't like the results, so he punched me straight in the nose. That did the trick, and I heard my os nasale fracture.

My eyes were watering so much that I couldn't see, but apparently Skinhead was either recharging his batteries, or the mobster had called him off.

"Yes," the Russian said. "So terrible about the Doctor. Good man. A freak auto accident from what I understand."

"Yeah, a real tragedy," I said, feeling no sympathy for the man who removed my eye. "I cried all night."

"So then, Mr. Sharp. You are going to tell me about your business with Rick Harris."

"Commodities," I said. "I wanted to start trading in commodities. That's what Rick Harris does. That's all. It's legit."

"Yes," The Russian said. "Zeus Investments. We did some looking into it...and into you, Mr. Sharp."

There was some signal exchanged, because Goatee turned and opened the large door into the room. It was dark inside and I couldn't see anything. He stepped in and disappeared. When he came out, he was dragging Naoko.

He dragged her into the room and dropped her in front of me. She was bound and had duct tape across her mouth. She was wearing her scrubs from the office. Her hair was mussed up, and she had some scratches on her left cheek. Her eyes were wild with terror, and puffy and red from crying. Goatee ripped the duct tape off.

"Jack!" she cried.

"Naoko!"

I tried to turn my head to see the Russian, but he was too far behind me.

"My associates came to pay you a visit," the Russian said. "Instead, we found her in your condominium. Most fortunate I say. Don't you Mr. Sharp?"

"Let her go!" I yelled. "She has nothing to do with this or Rick Harris! Let her go you mother fuckers!"

Internally, I was cursing myself more than them. My poor relationship skills had driven her into breaking up with me, and heading to my place to clear out her things, getting her caught up in my crazy life in the process.

"Let her go!" I yelled louder.

"Mr. Sharp, you are in no position to give orders."

"I'll fucking kill you if you hurt her!" I hissed.

"...or to make threats Mr. Sharp."

Goatee apparently thought this was funny, and started to chuckle.

"Jack!" she cried out again. "What's happening Jack?"

Goatee put the duct tape back across her mouth and dragged her away. He shoved her through the open door, and back into the dark abyss. The door closed with a loud thud.

"You mother fucker!" I screamed. "Let her go!" I was bouncing wildly on the chair trying to get out, but it was fruitless.

"We will Mr. Sharp," the Russian said. "As soon as you tell me what is really going on with Rick Harris. You see, if anyone else were to tell me they were investing in commodities, I would probably believe them. But you are much more complicated Mr. Sharp. Nothing is so simple with you."

I sat there panting, my initial fear replaced with rage and a bloodthirsty desire to kill.

"So now you will tell us, yes."

I took a deep breath.

"...or, the girl..."

He let his voice trail off.

I took a deep breath and exhaled, some drops of blood were blown off of my upper lip.

"Sabotage," I said finally. "Rick Harris has someone on the inside of an oil refinery."

"Very good Mr. Sharp. That's better. Now then, which oil refinery?"

"Champion Oil, the big one in Torrance. Rick Harris buys a futures contract for gasoline, he's got a person on the inside who monkeys around with stuff, and the place goes down. The price of gas on the spot market spikes, and he makes money on the spread. There, I said it – now let her go."

"Not so fast Mr. Sharp," the Russian said. "I find it hard to believe you would invest in such a thing, even if it could make you lots of money. It is too conventional for a man like you. What is your angle?"

"What my angle always is," I said. "Blackmail. Rick Harris thinks he controls the guy on the inside, but I've already compromised him. I've got about a ton of dirt on him, and he won't do anything unless I give the go-ahead. No valves get turned, no pumps get shutdown - unless I say so. Rick pays me off if he wants this thing to go down. He just doesn't know it yet."

"This man inside Champion, what is his name Mr. Sharp?"

"Fuck you," I said. "Not until the girl is released. Besides that, you couldn't compromise him like I have. If you want to play in the game, you have to work with me."

The Russian started to move behind me, pacing. I could hear the soles of his shoes on the wooden plank floor. His step was out of rhythm. I wondered if he had been kneecapped at one point in his colorful career. When he stopped walking, he started to speak again.

"I like blackmail Mr. Sharp," the Russian said wistfully. "I used to do it myself in the old country – but I like sabotage even more. Very ingenious plan you have. As always, you are a thorough man, and very resourceful."

"I am going to tell you how this is going to work Mr. Sharp. I am an old man, and I am too tired for the rough games I used to play. I need to start making money in a more conventional manner, a conventional manner with a slight twist. You will tell me when the sabotage is going to occur so I may order a futures contract. You will give your order to allow the sabotage to occur, and then afterward, you will turn over to me the name of the man inside Champion, and all of your evidence against him and Mr. Harris. They will start working for me."

"Okay," I said. "It's a deal. Now let the girl go."

"I think I will keep her around as a little insurance policy."

"I get her back when the refinery goes down," I said firmly. "Or it's no deal."

Skinhead was a man who abhorred a sassy tone with his boss, and he moved forward to wallop me again. This time Goatee stopped him with a big hand. Skinhead looked crushed.

"Again, you are in no position to bargain Mr. Sharp," the Russian reminded me. "But I am a fair man. I will bring the girl when you bring down the Champion Refinery. We can have a - what you call it – 'A Mexican Standoff.'"

" I saw that once in American movie," he laughed. "Very good. John Wayne I think. Do you like John Wayne, Mr. Sharp?"

Before I could answer my face was covered again with the chloroform soaked rag by Goatee. I smelled its sickening sweet aroma, and began to fade out. A shoot out with the Duke was the last thing I remembered.

THIRTY-ONE

The first thing I saw when I came to was a white sticker that read: "Driver carries only $20.00." I leaned forward and looked through the perforated clear Plexiglas barrier that separated me from the front seat. I saw a couple of freeway signs pass, and figured out that we were on the Harbor Freeway southbound.

"Where are you taking me?" I asked with a voice that was slurred.

The taxi driver, an Armenian based upon the name on his license, handed me a slip of paper. It read:

"Driver will take you back to your car Mr. Sharp. The rest is up to you. Don't fuck up or you will never see girl again."

I felt nauseated and closed my eyes.

* * *

Forty minutes later we arrived back at Naoko's condo. I was glad to see that my car was still there and hadn't been impounded as evidence of a violent crime. I swept the glass from the shattered side window off of the front seat with my hand and climbed in. I fished the keys out of my pocket and stuck them in the ignition. I didn't switch the car on.

"What the fuck are you going to do now One Eyed Jack?" I asked myself.

I had never actually intended to have the Champion Oil Refinery shut down. I would have had enough dirt on the three principles, based upon their recorded phone conversations, to lean on them. Now, the Russian had dashed those plans and added a new wrinkle to the whole affair. If I ever wanted to see Naoko alive again, I would have sit idly by while they went through with it.

Or would I?

I looked at my watch; it was 4:45 in the afternoon. I pulled out my phone and activated the GPS tracker in Nate Walker's phone. I could see that he was on his way in to work the night shift at Champion. I called him and he picked up immediately.

"Hullo."

"Mr. Walker," I said. "What time do you get off tomorrow morning?"

"Bout five-thirty or so."

"I'll be there waiting. We need to talk."

"Bout what?" he asked suspiciously.

"You are going to tell me all about the inner workings of the Champion Oil Refinery."

"Okay," he said easily, as if he had to explain such things all the time.

I hung up, got out of the car, and went to the trunk. I removed a small suede leather case from a hidden compartment in the spare tire well, and went up to Naoko's condo. I had the lock picked and was inside in less than thirty seconds.

THIRTY-TWO

Marion Holtzinger and I sat in my van, in one of the overflow parking lots, across the street from The Champion Oil Refinery and its Main Crude Unit. Another parking lot for the employees butted up against the fence to the Unit. From our vantage point, we could see straight into the plant. It was an impossible steel jungle of columns, pipes, and electrical conduits. Anchoring the plant at one end, were furnaces "A' and "B". These were the heart of the unit, and this was the first step in refining the crude oil, by heating it to almost eight hundred degrees. Without these furnaces, and the fractured oil they produced, the rest of the plant would go down and no gasoline could be produced.

Amazingly, a simple seven-foot high cyclone fence with a "V" of barbed wire was all that separated the unit and the facility, from the outside world. Immediately after 9-11, concerns were raised about a possible terrorist attack against a US nuclear power plant. This was the misguided worry by those that were uninformed, and the real security experts knew otherwise. Nukes were more impenetrable and hardened than your typical military base, and it would take an army of terrorists with sophisticated weapons to pose any credible threat.

The real danger was an attack against any one of the thousands of refineries, or petrochemical plants, that existed in the United States. Physical barriers, such as fences, were typically weak and rarely electrified, and facilities relied on contract security forces no better equipped to deal with a real assault than your typical mall cop. Most auto impound yards had better security – at least they had vicious dogs roaming around.

Two days from now, at the market close, the gasoline futures contract for the current month would expire. This left ample time for word to spread that the refinery had shut down, and for the markets to react nervously with a price spike.

I had hacked into the computer network of Zeus Investments and had seen that Rick Harris and Bill Batty had collectively purchased five hundred call options, for a total of $150 thousand dollars in RBOB contracts. Besides the direct investments they had made, Rick also had shifted a large percentage of the client money he managed into the option contracts. This would ensure that everyone under the magical Zeus umbrella made a tidy profit, and that the German investment group FH-1 Capital would sit up and take notice. Rick Harris could almost smell the $50 million dollars he would soon be riding herd over.

The Russian had purchased options through Zeus as well, and through a bogus corporation. Even if the price went up only five cents, the amount of money all of them stood to make was staggering. The night shift had started several hours ago and the sky was dark, the plant bathed in an orange glow from the shadow-less high-pressure sodium lights. By now, all of the workers had finished their scheduled rounds, and were settling in for what they thought would be an easy shift. It was time to make a call. I dialed Nate Walker.

"Hullo."

"Do it," I said. "Exactly like we rehearsed."

"Okay."

I hung up and put my phone on speaker so Marion could hear. In a few seconds we heard the rapid string of beeps as Nate speed-dialed Bill's phone. Bill, midway through the second ring, picked up the call.

"What's up?" he said quickly.

"Bill, I got some bad news for ya," Nate drawled. "I won't be able to do that thing for you tonight."

"What!" Bill cried. "Why not?"

"Got me into an accident," Nate explained. "Other night at work; backed the company truck into a Supervisor's car. They was pretty pissed. Made me take a drug test and gave me three days off until they gets the results. They call it 'zero tolerance' or somethin. Can't step foot on the property until then."

"Shit!"

"Good news is," Nate went on as if his were the only problems. "I watn'd on any drugs, and so when them results come back, I get my three days back pay."

"Fuck your back pay!" Bill screamed. "I've got a shit-load of money on this trade. This has to go down tonight!"

"Well," Nate said slowly. "There's always that part of the fence around the property I told you bout that you get through. Maybe you could get into the plant and do it yourself."

Nate had pointed out a section of the fence to me just to the south of the unit that had a large tree growing over it. Champion Oil had wanted to trim it back for obvious security reasons, but had been blocked when it was discovered that a Costa's Hummingbird had built a nest in it, and given birth. Several local bird-watching groups had gotten wind of it and lobbied Champion to let the tree remain until the babies were weaned and off on their own. PETA had also jumped into the fray and threatened to create a public relations disaster for the Oil Company, and brand them as heartless killers, if they disturbed the nest.

I pointed to the section of fence for Marion's benefit, and she nodded. We both turned our attention back to the cell phone, as we waited for Bill to respond.

"Me?" Bill said incredulously. "Why should I do it? I'm paying you for this job, remember? Why don't you drive over there and climb over the fence and do it?"

"I would if I was home Bill," Nate said. Thing is, since I'm off an all, my wife wanted us to go up to Santa Barbara to visit her sister. Kinda like a little vacation. If you can wait a couple days, maybe when I get back to work, I'll do it then."

"No, you fucking idiot! It has to be tonight!"

"Well Bill," Nate drawled. "Like I said; the tree's still there..."

There was a deathly silence as Bill considered the idea.

"It's still there?" he asked Nate. "Just like it was?"

"Even bigger. They ain't gonna fuck with it till them little birdies fly the nest. Hey Bill, sure you can't wait a couple days? I could really use the money."

"No," was all Bill said, and then hung up on Nate.

Marion looked at me nervously.

"What do you think?" she said. "Will he do it?"

I tapped some soft keys on my phone, and set it down on the seat between us with the display facing up.

A few seconds later I said, "He'll do it."

I pointed to the display on the phone. It showed that the GPS tracking device in Bill's phone was active. It also showed that he was heading toward Champion Oil.

THIRTY-THREE

It seemed as if it took an incredibly long time for Bill to arrive. The truth was, he was getting here as fast as possible, and I could tell by his speed that he was breaking a few laws on his way to breaking an even bigger one.

When the GPS showed him about a half mile away, I switched on my camera, and aimed it toward the compromised section of Champion's chain link fence. I turned off the GPS tracker and punched a couple of keys on the phone.

"What are you doing now?" Marion asked.

"Deleting the outgoing call from Nate's phone, and the received call from Bill's"

"Why?"

"They'll check Bill's phone for past calls. If it shows he received a call from an employee of the company, they'll drag Nate into it, and we don't need that. Remember, the first rule of extortion is to be the one controlling the information."

Marion nodded.

"What about phone company records?" she asked. "Won't they still show a record of the call?"

"Very good, Watson," I joked. "The thing is, since I hacked their phones, all calls go through my phone. The records will show that Nate called me, and that I called Bill, and my phone is untraceable."

We both saw Bill's dark blue pickup truck coming up the street at the same time.

"...And speaking of phones," I said to Marion, as I handed a new one to her. "You're up next."

She took it with a hand that I noticed was shaking slightly, and took a deep breath.

"It's all programmed; just hit the green button and say it just like we practiced."

She nodded and took a deep breath.

Bill went through the entrance to the employee parking lot, circled around the other rows of cars, and backed his truck up to the overgrown tree and the fence. I zoomed in on his license plate and without taking my eyes away said, "Do it."

She took another deep breath and dialed. In a few seconds, the plant's Receptionist picked up. I could hear a muted part of the conversation begin just as Bill emerged from the truck.

"Champion Oil," a bored female Receptionist recited.

Marion went into overdrive.

"Oh my God," she screamed into the phone. "You have to stop this crazy man! I was at a gas station and overheard him complaining about gas prices and saying he was going to blow up your refinery. I followed him in my car and saw him pull into your parking lot, and climb over the fence. He might have a bomb. You have to stop him!"

This got the Receptionist's attention and she immediately perked up. In the meantime, Bill had climbed into the bed of his pickup, and was hauling himself over the branches of the tree.

"Okay Ma'am," she said calmly and slowly. "Tell me your name first."

"I don't want to be involved," Marion said. "I just want him stopped."

"Okay. Can you tell me where you saw him climb the fence?"

"On Crenshaw Boulevard. He pulled into the big parking lot and climbed up over a tree into your plant. Hurry up and stop him!"

"Calm down Ma'am," the Receptionist said. "I'm alerting our security now. I want you to stay on the line. I have some more questions to ask."

Without putting the phone on hold, we could hear the Receptionist as she informed the plant's security personnel of the situation via radio. She was going through the standard protocol for bomb threats, which occurred routinely when the price of gas skyrocketed.

Bill was inside the fence and heading into the unit at a half trot. He disappeared into the mass of pipes and equipment, and I lost him.

The Receptionist came back on the line.

"Ma'am, can you please give me your telephone number in case we get disconnected. Marion looked over to me and I made a chopping gesture across my neck.

"I don't want to get involved," she said to the Receptionist and then hung up abruptly.

I gave her a thumbs-up, and made a mental note to get her a SAG card when this was all over.

A couple of white pickup trucks, I knew to be plant security, pulled up at the far end of the unit a few moments later.

I picked up my phone, switched on the app that simulated poor cell reception, and dialed the Torrance Police Department. As soon as the Dispatcher came on, I went into my spiel.

"Hi. I was just driving past the Champion Oil Refinery and I saw a man climbing the fence to get in."

"I'm sorry sir," the dispatcher said. "The reception is kind of bad. Did you say you saw someone climbing the fence into the Champion Oil Refinery?"

"Yes."

"What did you say sir?"

"I said yes!" I yelled louder. "He climbed over the fence from the parking lot on the Crenshaw Boulevard side."

"Crenshaw Boulevard did you say?"

"Yes. The parking lot."

"Ok sir. We're sending a unit now. I need to get some more information. Can you possibly –"

I pressed a button that increased the level of distortion, and then let the call drop. I switched on a police scanner that I had set to the Torrance PD frequency, and heard the call go out.

"Five-seventeen, investigate a possible trespassing at the Champion Oil Refinery. Report that a man climbed over the fence from the parking lot on the Crenshaw Boulevard side."

A few seconds later, a response to the call came in from one of the units.

"Five-seventeen, responding from Torrance and Western."

"Roger five-seventeen," the dispatcher repeated. "Show you to Champion Oil from Torrance and Western."

Just then, Marion and I saw Bill Batty streaking toward the perimeter fence and the overhanging tree. Two security personnel in light blue uniform shirts and black Dickies, were running after him. Even though they appeared out of shape, they caught up with him just as he was reaching for some low-hanging branches. They doubled up on him and dragged him down to the ground. But Bill wasn't giving up without a fight, and a scuffle ensued.

At the same time, a Torrance Police cruiser entered the lot with two officers in it. As soon as they saw the melee on the other side of the fence, they cut across the lot and raced up to scene. We heard the scanner crackle back to life.

"Any units to back five-seventeen at the Champion Oil Facility. Alleged trespasser is engaged in altercation with plant security personnel. Dispatch, notify Champion Oil security that we will be rolling additional units into facility."

"Roger, five-seventeen. Backup units to enter plant at gate three-A. Champion security being notified of situation"

A couple of other units responded and were racing to the scene. The initial officers had by now gotten out of their car, and were yelling commands to Bill to stop fighting and give up.

"Why don't they pull out their guns?" Marion asked.

"Too dangerous," I said, as the backup units raced past us, with their lights on and sirens wailing. "They won't shoot into the fence and risk the lives of the Security Guards unless they have no other choice."

Slowly, Bill disengaged with the security personnel and raised his hands up over his head. Marion and I watched as he first knelt and then laid on the ground facedown. Then one of the security personnel put handcuffs on his wrists. Once they were on, the other security guard kicked Bill in the side. The cops turned away as though they didn't see it.

Marion looked at me.

"Do you think he was able to bring down the unit before they got him?" she asked.

"No." I said. "I had our man on the inside rig the valves so they wouldn't close. He never had a chance."

THIRTY-FOUR

I had told Marion Holtzinger that once she made the phone call to the refinery and Bill was apprehended, she could leave the rest to me. But, she had insisted on seeing things through to the end, and I wasn't about to deny her that. We finally compromised that I would follow things here, and then meet her later at the Torrance Police Station. During all of the confusion with other police units arriving, and Bill being led away, I sent her off with instructions to grab a cup of coffee somewhere near the station, and that I would phone her later to come and meet me there. I hadn't told her about my run-in with the Russians, and didn't want her involved.

A few of the units lingered for a short while, shooting the breeze in the parking lot before finally heading off to start writing reports. As soon as everything was clear and calmed down, I made a call to the Russians.

"It's all set to go down," I said.

"We're on our way," was the response.

"Don't forget the girl," I said. "Or it's no fireworks."

I know they heard me, but they hung up without responding.

While I was waiting for them to arrive, I packed away my camera and scanner, and then made another call to Nate.

"In about a half hour Mr. Walker," I said very officially. "Be ready."

"I am," he said, just as officially.

The two Russian thugs pulled up in their car about thirty-five minutes later. I didn't see Naoko in the car with them. As soon as they got out I said, "The girl."

"In the trunk," Skinhead said.

"Get her out," I demanded.

"Fuck you," Goatee said.

I held up my phone. "She gets out of the trunk and into my car or it's no call. No call means no fireworks. No fireworks means no money for your boss. No money means your boss is going to be real pissed at you two for fucking this whole thing up, and losing him lots of money...do you want to do that?"

They looked at each other and then Goatee nodded to Skinhead. He stepped around to the back of their car and popped the trunk. He lifted Naoko out as if she were no heavier than a down pillow, and removed the handcuffs from her wrists, and the duct tape from her mouth. She ran towards me.

"Jack!" she cried and fell into my arms. I wrapped them around her and squeezed her as tight as I ever had. She was sobbing and I worked to calm her.

"It's okay..." I kept repeating. "...It's okay...You're safe now..."

Her body shook in my arms, and she felt very small and childlike.

"Are you okay?" I asked.

Her head nodded in the crook of my shoulder.

"Did they hurt you?"

She shook her head no.

"Enough!" Skinhead said, separating us. "You do this now. We don't have all fucking night."

"Fuck you!" I said to him before turning my attention to Naoko. I wasn't about to be rushed, especially now.

"Get in my car," I said very slowly. "You'll be safe there. I'll be done here in just a minute."

Reluctantly, she broke away and climbed into the car. I dialed Nate Walker. As soon as he answered, I said, "Do it." And then hung up.

Goatee, Skinhead, and I turned our gaze toward the plant and waited. There was hardly any traffic at this hour, and we could hear the monotonous hum of the plant as it kept running. It seemed like an eternity and I could hear the Russians shuffling about on their feet and getting antsy. I sure hoped Nate knew what he was doing. Then...

A giant fireball at least a hundred feet tall erupted from one of the refinery's flare stacks, brightening the sky with an orange glow. At the same instant, we heard an incredibly loud rushing sound like a rocket taking off. Alarm bells started going off and we could see personnel racing into the plant from the Control Center.

I turned to Goatee and he nodded and even smiled; his face had an orange glow from the huge fireball. Skinhead's slick noggin looked like a ripened peach.

Goatee pulled his phone out and made a call. He said something in Russian that I didn't understand, and then handed the phone to me.

"Very good Mr. Sharp," I heard my Russian nemesis say. "Now you hand over evidence of others involved, and we are very good. Nice doing business with you. We meet again, da?"

"Nyet." I said and then handed the phone back to Goatee.

I fished a memory stick out of my pocket and handed it to him.

"It's everything," I said. "More than you'll ever need."

He looked at it for a second, and then stuck it in his pocket. He said a few more words to his boss and then closed his phone. He and Skinhead got into their car and drove away.

As soon as they were far enough away, I called Nate Walker again.

"The show's over Mr. Walker. You can turn off the fireworks."

"Okay," he said.

"You've done a great service to your country," I said very formally. "The government of the United States is indebted to you."

"Sure," he said modestly, and then added. "Do I get a medal or somethin?"

I hung up.

The plant upset, and all the fireworks, had been nothing more than a charade - special effects staged by Nate. A couple of key emergency valves were opened that sent flammable gas to the unit's elevated flare stack and created the fireball. The rushing sound was relief valves designed to open and bleed off pressure in an emergency. The alarms were a poisonous gas detection system that Nate triggered manually. In the end, the Champion Oil Refinery never missed a beat, and would continue producing gasoline right on track. They would pay a fine for releasing gas into the atmosphere and would launch an investigation of the incident that would reveal nothing, but that would be the end of it. Nate may have been a screw-up with his finances and his vices, but he had intimate knowledge of how an oil refinery worked.

The fireball extinguished itself and the sky grew dark again. A second or two later, the roar from the relief valves stopped. I could see the workers out in the plant, milling around confused and annoyed, before returning to the safety and comfort of the Control Center to finish out their shift.

They were done with excitement for the night, but my work was just beginning. It was close to midnight, and the way I figured it, I would have about twelve hours or so before the Russians knew they had been had. Several news sources and internet sites carried current information about refining capacity and upsets at plants. Champion Oil would be conspicuously absent from any news and would report out that they were still producing on schedule. The memory stick I gave to Goatee had some secretly recorded phone conversations on it, but they were from a couple of characters planning a Ponzi scheme that I had leaned on several years back. Rick Harris and Nate Walker were nowhere to be found. I had to act fast.

I got into the car. Naoko was sitting there in a state of confused shock. She turned towards me.

"Who are you Jack?"

THIRTY-FIVE

"Never mind about that right now Naoko. What's more important is that you have to leave."

"What?" she said.

"Those guys will be back Naoko, to kill me, and to kill you."

She threw her hands up, exasperated.

"Jack! What is going on? Who are you, a spy?"

"No. I'm nothing like that. And right now, I'm the guy who cares very much for you, and the guy who is going to save your life. But you have to do exactly as I say Naoko."

"Jack...I..."

"Damn it!" I said, grabbing and shaking her. "Listen to me!"

I pulled out a manila envelope and handed it to her.

"Inside here is a plane ticket. It's a one way ticket to Hawaii. Your plane leaves out of Los Angeles International Airport in about three hours. You have to be on that plane Naoko. There's also a paper with some very important numbers printed on it, including bank account numbers and passwords. There's plenty of money in the accounts to tide you over. In the meantime, there's also a couple of thousand dollars in large bills in here."

I fished a set of car keys out of my pocket, and handed them to her. I gestured to a silver car parked at the end of the lot.

"The silver Acura. Return it to the Enterprise rental lot. It's already paid for. Take the shuttle over to the airport to catch your flight. I've packed up as many of your things as I could think of to bring over; they're in the trunk. All the rest of your stuff is being shipped over and should arrive in about a week. The tracking number is also on the paper. When I think it's safe, I'm going to re-register your car and have it shipped over."

All the talk was making her dizzy. She appeared close to becoming physically ill. I had to keep her intact. I handed her a cell phone.

"Here's a new phone. All of your numbers are transferred over. It's an untraceable phone, but be very careful who you give the number out to."

She stared at the phone in her hand, turning it over and over.

"What about my work Jack?" she said. "What about my friends? What do I tell them? I can't just disappear."

"Tell them that one of your parents is sick, and that you had to go home unexpectedly. You're going to have to take an extended leave of absence from work, and you don't know when you can return."

She looked up at me with a hard gaze.

"Can I ever return Jack?"

"Yes," I promised. "But not for a while. I promise I'll keep you informed."

THIRTY-SIX

"George Freeman to represent Bill Batty," I said to the Desk Sergeant.

He was sitting behind a sheet of bulletproof glass at the main reception area for the Torrance Police Department, and had a Sudoku book on top of some stacks of official papers. He deftly slid it under the papers.

"ID."

I fished out my wallet and slid a counterfeit California Drivers License, and matching BAR Card, through a slot in the window. He wrote down the information on a form and then slid them back to me.

On the way over, I had been concerned that Bill's wife had found a mouthpiece for him, and that they had already arrived and were inside the interviewing cell, and conspiring for his release and exoneration. Apparently, either she had not, or he had not yet arrived.

A few minutes later, another Officer was escorting me down a long hall toward the interview rooms. This place had the look and smell of every other Police Station I had been in – bare, cheerless walls, and with the smell of sweat, testosterone, and bad coffee.

On one side of the hall, were a set of doors labeled "one" through "four." The officer unlocked the thick steel door numbered "three" and pushed it open for me. Bill Batty sat on the other side of the bulletproof glass dividing the tiny room.

He looked tired and beaten. His face had some scratches on it from the scuffle at the refinery, and his eyes were puffy and red. I set my briefcase on the counter that butted up to my side of the glass, pulled out the plastic chair, and sat down. He looked me over and made a special point of staring at my eye patch. Something in his expression changed.

"So you're here to represent me?" he said.

"No," I said, returning his gaze. "I'm here to represent Marion Holtzinger."

That did it. A scowl erupted on his face.

"You!" he said. "You mother fucker! You're the guy that – "

"You're right Billy-Boy," I said, cutting him off. "I'm the one who's been dogging you. I know about the goings-on at The Peacock. I know about you pinching Marion every month for some spending money. I know about your slacker money-runner...but I also know about this."

I opened my briefcase and pulled out a digital recorder. I hit play and soon my recordings of the conversations between Bill and Rick Harris, and Bill and Nate Walker, filled the tiny room. I hit a button on the recorder and the room went silent. Bill was visibly stunned.

"Commodities manipulation, sabotage, domestic terrorism – where do you want me to start Bill?" I said. "Oil refineries are considered strategic assets of the United States, part of the critical infrastructure. I'm sure the Department of Homeland Security, the FBI, and every other law enforcement agency under the sun would like to hear about your little plan. They'd love to make a spectacle out of you to parade on the national news, and get some more money for their agencies."

His shock turned to rage and he gritted his teeth, hissing between them.

"You'll never live to see tomorrow you son of a bitch!" he swore. "Life is cheap if you know the right people. I'll have your ass killed!"

Slowly I turned the recorder in my hand so that the display was pointed toward him. A red light was on, indicating it was recording.

"Oh, I'm sorry Bill. I must have hit the wrong button. That last bit about you having me killed must have been recorded. I guess we can add 'conspiracy to commit murder' to the laundry list of your troubles"

I played it back for him and he heard his own desperate voice making impotent threats.

"The truth is, it doesn't matter if you have me killed Billy. Do you think I only have this dirt on a single recorder, in a single place? Welcome to the digital age caveman. These recordings, and the videos of you, and the e-mails that I have, all are backed up on secure servers out on the cloud. If I don't log into those servers and disable a program every two weeks, e-mails and videos start getting sent out."

I pulled out some sheets of paper and held them up to the glass for him to see.

"Here are all of your wife's e-mail contacts Billy. All of her stuffy socialite friends, her Garden Club, and her "Save the Dolphin" members. Do you think she'll be happy if they find out that her husband is a criminal...and a philanderer? She'll drop you like a bad habit, and then your problems will just begin. I know you signed a pre-nup with her when you got married. All that dough you thought you would have, to put up a brilliant defense, will be gone. You'll be stuck with a disinterested, overworked Public Defender trying to fight off the federal fucking government!"

I paused for a while to let it sink in. Already, he was looking down and avoiding my stare. He looked like he had shrunken several inches in a matter of minutes.

"Oh, and Billy," I continued. "Don't think I won't have a similar conversation with Rick Harris and Nate Walker. Do you seriously think they'll take one for you? The DA would have a field day with this one; everybody would be so busy ratting each other out to save their own skin, he won't know which way to turn. He'll get elected Mayor, and you'll be fighting to keep your booty virgin.

You are fucked Billy Boy, every fucking which way you turn"

He was quiet and staring into his hands. I couldn't tell if he was crying, but he might have been. The tough guy image was gone, along with any residual fight that might have been there. After a long time, he looked back up at me.

"What do you want?" he finally asked.

THIRTY-SEVEN

As I was passing back through the reception area of the Police Department to head to the parking lot, I overheard a man at the glass partition say, "Sam Goldman to represent Bill Batty."

The Sergeant looked up and saw me.

"Hey, I thought you were here for Bill Batty?" he said.

"He already fired me," I said, and continued out the door to the parking lot.

A faint glow was coming from the east, signaling the beginning of a new day. It had been a crazy past couple of days, and I wasn't done yet. I pulled out my cell phone and logged into an account I had set up to track Naoko's new cell phone. The GPS showed that she hadn't gotten cold feet, and had driven to the car rental lot before heading to the airport. At 2:41 a.m., about the time they would have been closing the aircraft doors, and pushing away from the gate, she had switched it off as per FAA regulations. She was asleep somewhere over the Pacific right now.

I spotted Marion's car in the parking lot, and leaned down to the passenger side window and tapped on the glass. She had nodded off and I startled her. The lock popped up and I climbed in. The car felt warm and inviting.

"Sorry," she said. "I dozed off."

I nodded sympathetically, and then turned toward her.

"It's over Marion," I said. "Your nightmare is finally over."

She let out a huge breath of air that she had been waiting to expel for months. Still, she had to be sure.

"Really over?" she said in a choked voice. "Completely over?"

"Over. Finished. Bill knows all the stuff I have on him, and he knows there's no way out. His Attorney is on his way in to see him right now, and I told Bill to let him know about everything. Attorneys are smart. He'll know immediately that we've got them by the balls. He'll tell Bill to do exactly as we say, and not to try to screw around."

"What will they charge him with?" Marion asked.

"The plant security never saw Bill trying to close the valves, so they can only go after him for trespassing, and maybe malicious mischief. He and his Attorney will concoct a story that Bill was trying to sneak in to take pictures of safety violations in the plant to use as leverage at the next Union contract negotiations. Even though he resigned his position with the union, Bill still has connections there. It would make for a plausible story and without any evidence - my evidence - to prove otherwise, that's all the DA would be able to charge him with. Remember, we still live in a country where you are innocent until proven guilty."

"Except with you Jack," Marion said wryly, and we shared a laugh at my expense.

"In the end," I continued. "They'll reduce the charges and let him off with a slap on the wrist, and maybe some community service. Look for him to be picking up trash, on the side of the freeway, in an orange jumpsuit, in a couple of months."

Marion laughed, and then looked down at her hands and asked in a voice that was very quiet.

"No more having to have sex with him then?"

"No, and no more payments. And, he's going to pay back all of the money he extorted from you - times ten."

She fell towards me, and burst into tears, her body shuddering. I put my arms around her.

"Thank you," she kept repeating. "Thank you...thank you...I never thought this would end."

I held her tightly in my arms and stroked her hair, soothing her. After a while, she took a deep breath and pulled back, although a bit reluctantly. I was reluctant too. She stared straight ahead through the windshield of the car, seeing nothing. She wiped the tears off her face with the back of her hand. She was quiet for a long time. Finally...

"Will I ever see you again Jack?" she asked, without facing me.

"No," I said. "You won't. I have other issues to attend to now."

She bit her lower lip and nodded slowly.

"But you'll still be out there watching won't you?"

"Yes," I said. "I'll still be out there watching."

She turned towards me and smiled.

"I like that," Marion Holtzinger said.

Jack is back!

One Eyed Jack is on the run and engaged in a deadly cat and mouse game with his Russian nemesis as the mobster attempts to track him down and kill him. Surviving by his cunning and street smarts, he must return to his painful past, and to the only person who can help him find his arch enemy and stop him for good.

"Russian Roulette" – A One Eyed Jack Novel

Available summer 2013

An excerpt:

From the inside of her car, I could see her striding purposefully across the parking lot, but without any cheer or conviction. Her head was high, but her face said she was a woman who had lost everything. When she was about twenty feet away, she pressed the key fob and the door locks popped up. I slid down further into the well behind the front seat and waited.

Inside the car, I could hear her drop her purse onto the passenger seat. Keys jiggled on a ring. As soon as the engine started, the door locks pulled closed. She put her seat belt on and I made my move.

"I won't hurt you," I said as I sat up behind her.

Instinctively, she undid her seat belt and reached for the inside door handle – which I had already removed.

"It's not there," I said. "And the door locks have been disabled."

She tried them - just to be sure - and then her thumbs pressed hard on the middle of the steering wheel.

"And the horn, and the panic button on your key fob – they're all disabled. You have to do as I say. Now just pull out, drive your normal route home and everything will be all right."

Reluctantly, she backed us out of the parking space without destroying any other cars and started heading south on La Cienega Boulevard. It was her usual route home.

"I...I don't have much money," she said in a cracked voice.

"I know. I don't want money. I just want information."

She ran a red light; by design, habit or from nerves I couldn't tell.

"Stop that," I said. "And slow down."

"I always drive this way."

"Not today. Turn left up here."

"That's not the way I –"

"Turn left," I commanded.

She complied and I had to remind her again to slow down.

I felt the car nose down slightly as she reduced speed. We were heading up into the

Baldwin Hills, an upscale area populated by well-to-do African-Americans. Soon, we had settled into a sedate speed amongst the hordes of cars making their way home.

"I want to know about your late husband," I said.

She took a slow, deep breath through her nostrils and I noticed her hands grip the wheel a little more tightly.

"Why do you want to know about him?" she asked, with a hint of irritation.

"He took something from me," I said.

She snorted. "He took a lot of things from people."

I shifted in the back seat so that she could see my face in the rearview mirror.

"Not this," I said and raised the eye patch over my left eye, revealing my empty socket.

She screamed and I had to grab the wheel to avoid a head on collision.

ABOUT THE AUTHOR

Christopher Lynch is a Southern California native and a freelance writer living in Los Angeles. Besides fiction, he enjoys writing on a variety of subjects.

He is also an avid cyclist and a mountain climber with successful summits of Mount Whitney, Mount Shasta, Mount Kilimanjaro in Africa, Mount Kalapatar in Nepal, and has recently completed a trek to Mount Everest Base Camp.

He counts as one of his greatest accomplishments the successful training and leading of nine blind hikers to the summit of 10,000 foot Mount Baldy, the highest point in Los Angeles County and the third highest peak in Southern California. A documentary film is being made of the adventure and you can view a trailer at: http://www.baldyfortheblind.com

He is a member of Sisters in Crime Los Angeles Chapter and the Children's Book Writers and Illustrators of Los Angeles.

You can view more of Chris's writing at his website: http://www.christopherjlynch.com

18189532R10144

Made in the USA
San Bernardino, CA
04 January 2015